STILL MORE
OF THE BEST

Still More of the Best

Stories for Girls

Formerly LIKE IT IS

Edited by

N. Gretchen Greiner

Illustrated by

Jim Conahan

Cover by

Tom Nachreiner

GOLDEN PRESS

Western Publishing Company, Inc.

Racine, Wisconsin

Contents

An Introduction

What's So Special About Girls?

Girls are special in many ways, but one of the very nicest is in their taste in reading. Girls like variety. They want more than just adventure tales or stories about people in deadly danger— climbing the face of a mountain or tracking a vicious bear or fighting it out with the bad guys —you know the kind of thing. Girls want a story collection that lets them react in a lot of different ways to a lot of different characters in a lot of different situations.

As you turn these pages, you'll find all kinds of girls and problems (one of the girls may be you; one of the problems may be yours). Here and there, you may cry a little. Certainly you'll chuckle—even guffaw!—in many spots. You may

9

even get downright angry at some of the girls and the ways they deal with their troubles. One thing is sure: You'll enjoy *Still More of the Best* because it has some of everything.

Here are the girls you'll meet:

KAREN, faced with the destruction of her world as her parents contemplate divorce, finds that she can't even keep her beloved cat, who is about to have kittens—but then, along comes Pete.

TENA has to learn—but fast!—how to control a huge, spoiled dog who's a real delinquent. In the process, she learns how to handle her problems with a boy and a scholarship.

CLARE, bitter and withdrawn after her hand is mutilated, is forced, when Jon needs her friendship and understanding, to stop thinking only of herself.

ANNE discovers, in the hardest way of all, that teachers are people—very real people, with interesting personal lives and intense personal feelings.

VESTA and SALLY B., so much alike and yet so different, must fight each other's prejudice, as well as their own, to preserve the friendship they both treasure and need.

DARLENE's highly unsatisfactory love life is set right only after her young brother takes to tossing a pair of raw chickens hither and yon—and finally in the direction of a new boy.

LORNA, an only child, is smugly comfortable and self-centered. Suddenly confronted with the prospect of a new baby in the house, she's sure that her life is shattered—until her friend, knee-deep in younger siblings, gives her something to think about.

KARRY learns to love unselfishly when Lang teaches her that it's best to set free the object of her love.

DEBBIE discovers that she must grow out of being a typical teen-ager—and do it all in a single day. She does it, too, while concealing from her mother the tragic reason for her decision.

DEBBIE, another and very different teen-ager, keeps her life and everybody else's in a turmoil because of her addiction to "rights." Her running feud with the high school principal over dress is the stuff of which legend is made.

So—there are the girls and the situations in *Still More of the Best*. Turn the page and see how they all turn out!

N.G.G.

Good-Bye, Miss Kitty

Jane L. Sears

KAREN NERVOUSLY TIGHTENED her hands on the handlebars as she steered her bike boldly past the NO TRESPASSING sign at the top of the road. What if someone saw her and ordered her off this private land that was part of the Forresters' big ranch? She couldn't say she was a friend of Pete's, because she really wasn't. Blond and dreamy-looking and sixteen, Pete Forrester didn't know a lowly ninth-grader like Karen Cummings was even alive.

Well, why worry about it? There wasn't anyone in sight, and in a few minutes her dreadful mission would be over and done with, and she would be gone.

Swallowing hard against the sudden lump in her throat, Karen braked to a stop, anxiously scanning the scene below. What a beautiful sight it was! Sun poured like liquid gold through the graceful poplar trees, bathing the big white house and red barn in its warm summer glow. Beyond were rolling hills and lush pastures dotted with sheep and grazing cows. Barking amiably at their heels was Pete's Irish setter, Muldoon.

"Oh, golly!" Karen groaned aloud. "I forgot all about Muldoon."

Then she remembered how good-natured and friendly the setter was, always wagging his tail and letting the kids pet him when he waited for Pete after school. In fact, Karen suspected that the setter and Miss Kitty might become very good friends. With all her heart she hoped so. Miss Kitty was certainly going to need a friend when she realized her own mistress had cruelly abandoned her.

Karen looked at the gray and white cat curled contentedly in the basket attached to the handlebars. Her heart ached at the look of trust in those big green eyes and the soft mew that seemed to say, "I love you." How could Karen

14

make Miss Kitty understand?

"This is going to be your new home now." Karen choked as she lifted Miss Kitty into her arms. "The Forresters will love you a lot, and when they see that you're going to have baby kittens in a week or so. . . ."

Her voice faltered away on a sob. She mustn't break down, not now, Karen scolded herself. There would be time enough for tears back home when she put away her pet's silly toys and soft blankets—just as she was putting Miss Kitty away now, out of her life, forever.

Miss Kitty was nuzzling her whiskery face against Karen's cheek. After one last convulsive hug, Karen put her down and said firmly, "I have to go now, so this is good-bye. Just follow that path, all the way down to the house. Well, go on!"

Ignoring the sharp command, Miss Kitty proceeded to wash her face with one paw, pausing now and then to watch a blue jay scolding from a tree. After a moment, her tail moving like a graceful plume, she walked over to rub herself against Karen's ankle.

"No, you can't come with me!" Karen scolded and pushed Miss Kitty away with her foot.

15

She saw the stunned look on the cat's sweet, gentle face before she jumped on her bike and rode away.

Karen didn't dare to look back. She didn't have to turn her head to know that Miss Kitty was standing there watching after her, mewing in bewilderment.

Blinded by tears and tormented by the empty basket, Karen pedaled faster and faster. Memories chased her, flashing across her mind like pictures on a screen. She saw Miss Kitty as a lost, sick kitten huddled on the porch that stormy night two years ago. Love, feedings through an eyedropper, trips to the veterinarian for shots and vitamins—those things had saved Miss Kitty from certain death.

She saw Miss Kitty that following Christmas, when the twinkling lights on the tree had startled the playful, half-grown kitten. She had hissed and arched her back in a hilarious imitation of defiant fierceness. Other memories, too, haunted Karen's mind: Miss Kitty perched on Karen's desk, head cocked, little paw batting at the pen as it scratched out pages of homework; another of Miss Kitty, silent and solemn this time, because Karen was sick in bed with the flu. . . . But now it was over, and she would never see Miss Kitty again.

Suddenly there was the roar of a motor, then an angry yell from the road behind her. "Hey! Wait a minute, you crazy girl! You forgot your cat!"

Startled, Karen ran her bike into a rut, pitched sideways, and fell, sprawling, into a ditch. And that's when she saw Pete, on his Honda, with a terrified and struggling Miss Kitty tucked beneath his arm.

"Hey, are you hurt?" Pete was off his Honda and at her side before she could pick herself up. When she did, red-faced and embarrassed, she saw his blue eyes flicker over her admiringly and was suddenly glad she'd worn her best white slacks and red blouse, with a matching ribbon holding back her long, dark hair.

"I—I'm all right, I guess," she murmured unsteadily. "Just kind of dusty, that's all."

He was still staring at her, his blond head tipped to one side, when he said, "I've seen you around school, haven't I? Your name is Carol—Caroline. . . ."

"Karen. Karen Cummings."

"Sure! Now I remember. Say, this is some tiger

you've got here. I'm glad I caught you before you got too far.''

Miss Kitty, wildly clawing at Pete's arm, was trying to get to her mistress. When Karen ignored her cat, Pete's eyes narrowed suspiciously.

"Hey, you didn't forget this cat; you brought her up here to dump her, didn't you?" he accused. When Karen didn't answer, he thrust Miss Kitty at her, saying, "Man, what a crummy way to treat a helpless animal—a pregnant one, at that!"

"You don't understand. I—I had to," Karen protested, then dissolved into helpless tears. Now, with Miss Kitty back in her arms, she would have to go through the same painful parting all over again.

"Listen, please don't bawl!" Pete begged. "I didn't mean to yell at you." He looked flushed and concerned, like Daddy always did when Mother cried and carried on, and up close like this, Pete was so handsome that Karen's heart fluttered in her chest.

"I know you think I'm mean," Karen finally said, "but, you see, I can't keep Miss Kitty anymore, Pete. My parents are separated, and while Mother's in Mexico getting the divorce, I'll be staying with my grandmother in New York. The problem is, she isn't allowed to have pets in her downtown apartment."

Their eyes held for a long moment before Pete muttered, "Gosh, that's really rough—about your folks, I mean." He went over to sit on a low fence, chewing thoughtfully on a blade of grass before he said, "I don't know what I'd do if my folks decided to break up. They fight sometimes, but no matter how mad they get, they always work it out. I guess that's because they don't hate each other like your parents do."

Karen leaned against the fence beside him, her hand idly stroking the cat dozing peacefully in her arms. After a time she said, "That's just it. My parents don't really hate each other. In fact, I can tell they're still in love, but they're too stubborn to admit it."

She told Pete how bored and lonesome Daddy sounded on the phone since he had moved to his club a month ago and how Mother stared at their wedding picture all the time and cried and cried.

"Daddy is always asking me how Mother is, and Mother is always asking me how Daddy is, but when I ask them what's wrong, they both

19

tell me I'm too young to understand," Karen said.

Pete made a sound of disgust. "Wow, what a mess! I'll bet it's your mom's fault. Women always expect men to do all the apologizing. A man's got his pride, too, you know, and your dad is probably waiting for her to invite him back, unless—"

"Unless what?" Karen echoed anxiously.

"Well—" Pete's voice was reluctant—"unless he's got one of those secretaries with yellow hair and a build, like those homewreckers on TV, you know?"

Remembering her father's secretary, Karen gave a mournful little laugh. "Miss Phipps has gray hair, and she's as skinny as a rail. Besides, my mother has blond hair, and she's really beautiful. I've heard Daddy tell her so." She let out a long, unsteady breath. "No, it's more complicated than that. You see, Daddy has this job offer with a company way up in Alaska, but Mom refuses to leave. So they just decided to get a divorce."

"Grown-ups!" Pete groaned. "They're sure kooky sometimes. They tell us we're too young and too dumb to understand, but they're the

20

ones who act like unreasonable babies."

Suddenly Pete's fingers closed hard around Karen's shoulder. "If I were you, I'd go to my room, lock the door, and go on a hunger strike; and I wouldn't eat or come out until they get back together again. You've got some rights, too, you know."

"Oh, Pete, don't be silly!" Karen exclaimed. "What girl of fourteen has rights, anyway? Besides, I won't have a room much longer, because Mother has the house up for sale. I—I've never lived in another house, and pretty soon it'll belong to strangers. . . ."

This time Karen's tears failed to move Pete. In fact, they obviously annoyed him. He sneered, "Boy, are you ever a gutless wonder!" His cold eyes moved down to Miss Kitty, who had fallen asleep against Karen's shoulder. "Here your own home is breaking apart, and all you can do is bawl and run around trying to dump that poor pregnant cat!"

Each sarcastic word was like a knife in Karen's heart. She was too hurt to be angry. She panicked when a bell clanged in the distance and Pete said he had to go now because it was chow time.

21

When he started toward his Honda, Karen begged, "Pete, please take Miss Kitty! Because she's pregnant, no one in our neighborhood will have her, and if I take her to the S.P.C.A., she'll be given away to strangers—maybe even put to sleep. Won't you give her a home?"

He hesitated so long that Karen's heart sank to her toes, but it lifted when he said gruffly, "Okay, give her here. No—no slushy good-byes," he added when Karen started to kiss Miss Kitty's nose. "You gave her to me, remember?"

Then he had Miss Kitty in his arms, and Karen's were empty and aching. She could barely mumble a thank-you before the boy and the cat rode away, with Miss Kitty struggling and spitting as she looked back over Pete's shoulder.

On the way home, Karen tried to comfort herself with thoughts of Miss Kitty's wonderful new home, the love and attention she would get, and the fun she would have. But another thought kept intruding, and she couldn't forget Pete's cold, accusing eyes. Imagine his telling her to go on a hunger strike! Why, she wouldn't dare to pull a defiant stunt like that. Besides, she knew it wouldn't do any good, anyway.

Mother was packing china and silver in the

boxes that would be put into storage next week. Karen forced a smile when she joined her in the living room. She described the ranch and her meeting with Pete, then said, "I'm going to my room now; I'm tired, Mother."

"Karen?"

Mother rose from her knees and came over to take Karen in her arms. They stood that way for a long time, holding on to each other hard.

"I'm sorry about Miss Kitty, honey," Mother said thickly. "I know how hard all of this is on you, but someday—"

"I know!" Karen interrupted with a sob. "Someday I'll understand!" Then she ran to her room and threw herself on her bed, her throat so tight that it felt as if she were being choked by invisible hands. Later, when Mother tapped softly on the door, Karen pretended to be asleep but wondered if she would ever sleep again. Everywhere she looked she seemed to see Miss Kitty—on the bed, in the chair, on the window-sill. Would Pete fix a nice bed for Miss Kitty? she wondered with new worry. Or would he put her out in that drafty old barn to sleep? And when the kittens started to be born, would he know what to do?

23

Now, looking back, Pete seemed mean-tempered instead of friendly and the ranch wild and desolate rather than beautiful. And that Muldoon! Maybe he wasn't a gentle dog at all. Maybe behind those soft brown eyes there lurked a vicious, fang-toothed monster ready to chase a pregnant cat up a tree!

The days that followed were like a nightmare. Karen picked at her food during the silent meals and slept badly. A dozen times or more, she was tempted to call Pete to remind him that Miss Kitty liked to be fed twice a day and preferred milk to cream, but most of all, she yearned to know how her cat was. Only it wasn't her cat anymore. It was Pete's, and she knew he would resent any tearful interference.

People came to inspect the house daily, many of them complaining that it was too small, too big, or too old. After one woman made nasty remarks about the size of the living room, Karen said to her mother, "Do we have to sell it? Can't we two keep living here, even if Daddy doesn't? It's our *home!*"

Her mother's voice was barely audible when she replied, "It was a home, but, without your father, it's nothing anymore. Nothing!"

24

She quickly turned her head, but not before Karen saw the shine of tears in her eyes. "Please don't make it any more difficult for me than it already is, honey," Mother murmured brokenly. "I'm only doing what I know is right."

But it's not right! It's silly and stupid and wrong! Karen's heart cried. Still, she said nothing. What could she say that would do any good?

Three days before Karen was to leave for New York, Daddy called. "Hi, princess," he said, in that special warm voice. "How's my girl?"

"I—I'm fine," Karen lied. Then Mother took the phone, her cheeks flushed with excitement that didn't match her cool voice as she told Daddy that the movers would put the furniture in storage Tuesday, that the house hadn't been sold but she was going to let the realtor handle it, and that she and Karen would both be flying out Tuesday afternoon.

"Of course you can come by Monday night," she finally said. "Naturally Karen wants to say good-bye." There was a little pause, and then Mother said, "No, Frank, I have not changed my mind. Have you? . . . I see; then that's that!"

The packing continued, with Karen agonizing

25

over each chair, each lamp, each table. There were still little rips in the side of the couch, where Miss Kitty had sharpened her claws, and tiny teeth marks on a chair leg.

Every inch of the house, of every room, was so familiar, so dear, and so filled with memories of past happy times that Karen felt her heart would break. It had been such a warm, wonderful home, and in three days Karen would never see it again.

On Monday it began to storm. Rain lashed trees that quivered against the force of the wind. Thunder cracked while jagged streaks of lightning pierced the dark, angry clouds.

While Mother did some last-minute sorting in the attic, Karen packed her winter things in the trunks being sent to storage. When she was through, she went downstairs, pacing from window to door, her body shivering with each boom of thunder that shook the house. Was Miss Kitty frightened? Would Pete see her fear of storms and hold her in his arms? Oh, there were so many things he needed to know about such a sensitive cat, but Karen was afraid to call him— afraid to hear that Miss Kitty might still be miserable and lonesome without her.

She tried to shake the brooding thoughts away, reminding herself that Miss Kitty had been gone for two weeks now and had probably forgotten all about her.

Suddenly there was a rattling sound at the kitchen door. Daddy? But it was only three o'clock, and he'd said he wouldn't be over until he got off work at five. Knowing Mother would want to put on fresh lipstick, as she always did when he came, Karen called up to her, "Daddy's here! He's early!"

"Let him in, dear!" Mother answered. "I'll be right down!"

The rattling sound came again, and Karen ran to open the back door, calling, "I'm coming, Daddy!" She swung the door wide and saw no one on the porch. She unlatched the screen, stepped outside, then sucked in a shocked breath. Waiting there by the steps was a thoroughly drenched, skinny cat with bloody paws and a muddy coat—a mother cat holding a tiny, mewling kitten by the scruff of its neck.

"Miss Kitty?" Karen whispered unbelievingly. "Is it really you? It is! It *is* you—*Mother-r-r!*"

Karen heard her mother's gasp from behind her as, laughing and crying, she scooped up the two wet, furry bodies in her arms and carried them into the kitchen. There she lovingly deposited Miss Kitty and her baby on the throw rug, while Mother kept saying, "All this way, at least two miles. I can't believe it!"

It was true. Miss Kitty had found her way home again, and she'd carried her baby with her.

Mewing proudly, Miss Kitty kept rubbing against Karen's ankles while Karen knelt to wipe off the kitten with a soft towel. When Miss Kitty's bloody paws had been treated with ointment and she and her baby had been fed, she limped slowly to the back door and emitted a very determined, very impatient *Meow-w-w-w-w!*

As Karen and her mother exchanged a baffled look, Miss Kitty cried again, scratching at the door, her green eyes filled with anxiety as she gazed beseechingly at her mistress.

Just then there was a loud knock. Then an even louder voice demanded, "Hey, open up, Karen! Hurry, before they catch cold!"

This time it was Pete, his blond hair hanging in wet strips on his brow, and in his arms was a covered basket filled with the other four kittens of the litter!

"She had 'em last week," he explained breath-lessly, while Miss Kitty clawed, crying, at his leg. "When I found her and one of 'em gone a few hours ago, I suspected she might have come here, so I figured I better bring the others to save her any more trips. Whew!"

He put the basket down, and Karen watched incredulously as Miss Kitty took the kittens, one by one, in her mouth and carried them to the rug. When she was finished licking them all thoroughly, she curled herself around the fuzzy little bodies, her eyes narrowed to lazy slits of smug triumph. Dropping to her knees, Karen tenderly touched each tiny head before framing Miss Kitty's pansylike face between her hands. Although Karen had cruelly abandoned Miss Kitty, her love and devotion were so strong that she had brought herself and her family home again. With her whole being she was tell-ing Karen, *I belong to you, and I won't let you put me out of your life!*

Karen's eyes streamed with tears. She felt weak and, yes, gutless, compared to her coura-geous cat. She felt something else, too: a new strength and determination that made her rise to her feet and turn to face her mother.

30

"*I* won't be shoved around and—and *dumped off* on Grandmother, either!" she heard herself say. "Divorce is—is bad, and it's stupid, especially when two people still love and need each other the way you and Daddy do. Well, you can act like a couple of dumb kids, but Miss Kitty and I are staying right here, and that's that!"

Mother's face flushed with mounting anger. "That's about enough, young lady," she said coldly. "You don't understand—"

"But I do understand!" Karen insisted. "I understand that you and Daddy are wrecking three lives, and Miss Kitty's life, too, by breaking up your marriage. What does it matter if we live in Alaska or on the moon—so long as we're all together?"

"Atta girl," Pete muttered. "Now go lock yourself in your room and go on that hunger strike, just like I told you!"

Karen hardly heard him. She was still holding her mother's eyes, shaking and terrified inside at her rude defiance but determined to stand firm, because, in her heart, she knew she was right. Pete had helped her to learn that, and so had Miss Kitty.

Mother was looking at her in amazement, as

if she could scarcely believe that her obedient little girl would speak in such a way. She could still make Karen catch that plane on Tuesday, and in the tense silence, Karen saw the inner struggle going on in her mother's mind—before her mother suddenly turned to gaze down at Miss Kitty and her babies. Her sigh was long and relieved, as if some kind of terrible weight had been lifted from her shoulders.

She said, almost joyously and with a lovely smile, "You don't need to go on any hunger strike, Karen, because we're going to have too wonderful a dinner to miss." Hugging Karen hard, she added, "And you know something else? There isn't going to be any divorce—not anymore."

By the time Daddy arrived after work, there was a lemon pie cooling on the kitchen counter, a big frozen chicken thawing and browning in the oven, and a dining room glowing with warm candlelight that shone on crystal and silver.

"Welcome home, Daddy!" Karen laughed, throwing herself into his arms. She laughed again at the baffled look on his face as he took in the cheery sights and fragrant smells and the smiling, beautiful wife who turned from the stove to look into his eyes.

"Well, what's going on here?" Daddy said, his voice catching. "Where'd all those cats come from, and—who is that?" he added, grinning at Pete, who looked ridiculous in a frilly apron as he cut up lettuce for a salad. "Hey, have I walked into the wrong house?"

"No, dear," Mother said, coming over to link her arm through his. "You've walked into the right house—your *own* house—and when I've told you all about it, I think you'll want to stay."

Daddy answered, his eyes bright, "I think I already do. Yes, I'm sure of it, sweetheart."

Much, much later, after a wonderful dinner and when the dishes were done and Mother and Daddy were still talking in the living room, Karen and Pete stood in the kitchen looking down at Miss Kitty and her sleeping kittens.

"I can see why she wanted to come home to you, Karen," Pete said in a low voice. "You're quite a girl; do you know that?"

"I think I'm learning to be, thanks to you, Pete."

His blue eyes never left hers. "Any chance of us making a date to go swimming next Saturday afternoon—if it's a nice day, I mean?"

"I'd like that, Pete," she said, and they smiled

a little foolishly at each other.

Pete pressed her hand and was gone. Karen stood at the door, watching until the red taillight on his Honda disappeared from sight. The rain had stopped at last, and riding across the sky was a big full moon with a face that smiled down at her. When Miss Kitty came to rub against her ankle, Karen picked her up and pressed her cheek against the sweet, whiskery face, whispering, "Hello, Miss Kitty, hello, Miss Kitty," over and over again, because it was so wonderful to know that they would never have to say good-bye again.

Dog-Sitter

Carl Henry Rathjen

WHEN TENA TERRILL rang the doorbell that evening, she heard ferocious barking deep within the house. Then, despite a woman's shrill command, clawed feet scrambled, and a heavy body slammed so hard against the door that it seemed to bulge outward. Tena's heart raced nervously. She would have fled if she hadn't needed money so badly for veterinary college in the fall.

Amid the barking, she heard the woman's high-pitched voice again. "Quiet, Rowdy! Quiet!" The barking continued. "Down, Rowdy!" The raking of claws sounded as if the dog were trying to tear down the door. Tena gritted her teeth. Finally the door opened a crack. Two sets of noses and eyes peered out.

Tena spoke to the higher set. "Mrs. Mac-Gruder? I'm Tena Terrill, your dog-sitter."

"Oh, come in," said Mrs. MacGruder. "Down, Rowdy!" But when she opened the door wider, the big mass of woolly gray dog pulled her out on the porch as she clung to his collar. She was a thin, dark-eyed woman with red-dyed hair, dressed for a party, in a strapless silver evening gown. The dog would have yanked her off her feet if Tena hadn't caught her arm. "Rowdy!" Mrs. MacGruder chided, then smiled at Tena. "He's just boisterous. He means well."

"I'm sure he does," said Tena, tensely lowering her free hand so the dog could sniff it and get acquainted. Rowdy got too well acquainted; he closed his jaws on her hand. Tena stifled a little shriek.

"He won't hurt you," said Mrs. MacGruder. "My husband taught him that. Just don't try to pull your hand away."

Tena didn't want her fingers pulled off, so she just stood very still and looked down at the huge dog. It was hard to tell what breed predominated in Rowdy. The disheveled hair suggested sheep dog or, possibly, untrimmed French poodle.

What could be seen of the ears hinted at shepherd, though the broadness of the skull was more Newfoundland. At the moment, Tena wasn't particularly interested. She just wanted her hand back.

"Hi, Rowdy. Good boy. Let go."

Rowdy just hung on and growled, and from the depths of hair came an intent gleam of eyes. Tena tried to stare down the gleam while endeavoring to work her hand free, but the only response she got was another warning growl.

"Shall we go inside?" Mrs. MacGruder suggested pleasantly.

"I don't seem to have much choice," Tena remarked, following her hand as the dog carried it into the house. If she had been a little more tactful in announcing her choice of career to Mel Fortner's father, she thought bitterly, she wouldn't be in for the wild evening this promised to be.

With her free hand, she patted the dog's head, then casually slid her palm under the jaw. Her fingers pressed muscles on each side, and Rowdy abruptly released her hand—and just as quickly turned his head to close big jaws on her wrist.

A man's laugh boomed from the stairway. "That's the stuff, Rowdy. Show her who's boss." The ruddy-faced man coming down the stairs looked huge and uncomfortable in his tuxedo. He winked at Tena. "Pretty smart mutt, isn't he? Think you can handle him?"

Tena kept her doubts to herself. "I wouldn't have put the ad in the paper if I were afraid of dogs," she answered. At the time she'd written it, she'd thought the advertisement was pretty clever:

DOG LOVERS! KEEP YOUR DOG AND YOUR NEIGHBORS LOVING YOU. DON'T LEAVE YOUR DOG LONESOMELY BY HIMSELF TO ANNOY THE NEIGHBORS AS HE HOWLS AND BARKS FOR COMPANIONSHIP. KEEP PEACE AND HAPPINESS WITH DOG-SITTER TENA TERRILL.

Mr. MacGruder bellowed at Rowdy. "Leggo, mutt!" The big dog released Tena's wrist, whirled, and jumped at him. Mr. MacGruder cuffed Rowdy aside playfully, with a blow that would have sent most dogs, and men, whimpering. Rowdy barked ferociously and lunged again, tail wagging furiously.

Above the pandemonium, Mrs. MacGruder's voice shrilled. "That ad really caught our eye. It's a wonderful idea, and it was the perfect answer to our problem. We've been having all sorts of prejudiced complaints from neighbors. They've even called the police and—Mike!" she screamed at her husband. "I can't hear myself think, and if you're not careful, Rowdy's going to tear that suit!"

Mr. MacGruder grabbed a fistful of Rowdy's hair and clamped a huge hand over his jaws. He wrestled the growling dog to the floor.

"Just a warm-up for tonight," he said, grinning at Tena. "I'll be lucky if this suit's in one piece when I come home. Last year we had seven fights at the annual shindig!"

Mrs. MacGruder brought her voice down a couple of octaves; even so, it was shrill. "As I was saying, whatever gave you this wonderful idea of being a dog-sitter?"

"I had been a baby-sitter—" Tena began. But that was a tactless subject, especially if she mentioned that she'd lost her last regular job because the kids had been kept awake by a barking dog next door. That had been her alibi, though maybe she'd been partly to blame because of the row

39

with Mel—ending with giving him back his fraternity pin. "Well," she went on quickly to the MacGruders, "since I plan to become a vet, what better way is there to gain rapport with animals than dog-sitting?"

"Rap what?" Mike MacGruder demanded.

"I'll spell it out for you on the way to the ball," said his wife. She turned to Tena. "We can't stay as late as last year—seven o'clock in the morning, it was."

"Oh, no!" said Tena.

"Mike has to get some sleep before he goes on the road tomorrow morning. So we'll be in before midnight. There are soft drinks in the refrigerator and doughnuts in the cabinet alongside it. If I were you—you're so small and Rowdy's so powerful—I wouldn't take him for a walk if—"

At the mention of "walk," Rowdy erupted wildly from the floor. His exuberance caused a floor lamp to rock dangerously before Mike MacGruder casually steadied it.

"Oh," shrilled Mrs. MacGruder, "I shouldn't have said that word. But while we're on that subject, Tena, other words to be careful of are 'bone' and—"

40

Rowdy went berserk; a coffee table went over with a crash; Mike MacGruder cuffed Rowdy down. "Come on, hon; we'll be late."

One by one, the couple slipped out the front door, while Tena clung tenaciously to Rowdy's collar. He barked furiously. Tena couldn't quiet him but was hoping to succeed somehow, when the front doorbell rang. Rowdy went into orbit. Tena opened the door a crack, expecting to see irate neighbors—or maybe the police. Instead, it was Mrs. MacGruder.

"Sorry; I just remembered you said you're going to be a vet, so I needn't have come back to remind you not to give Rowdy any chicken bones from the refrigerator, need I?"

Tena couldn't reply. It would have been useless. The word "bones" drove Rowdy into a frenzy of barking and dashing back and forth through the house—to the kitchen, then back to Tena. She grabbed him and was dragged several feet as she commanded him to be quiet. The struggle went on. She wondered if it would be easier to straddle him and ride him, like a broncobuster, to a standstill.

"Don't lose patience," she warned herself, remembering the disastrous aftermath when she'd lost patience with Mel's father, a veterinary and a high-ranking member of the faculty at State, where Mel was taking his second year of veterinary medicine. She'd thought Mel's father would be pleased with her announcement that she hoped to win a scholarship and become a vet, too. Later, she and Mel could work together in their own animal hospital. Dr. Fortner had frowned, then told her not to expect him to use any influence in her behalf on the scholarship. He'd given the impression that he thought she was faking an interest in veterinary college only so she could chase after his son and interfere with his studies. Tena had set him straight so tactlessly that it had led to the row with Mel. Now Mel thought she'd been using him to get his father's influence for the scholarship.

So now Tena had no fraternity pin of Mel's, no chance of a scholarship, no chance of college if she didn't get enough money otherwise, and no chance of getting enough money if she couldn't make this spoiled brat of a big dog behave, so his owners would recommend her to other owners!

Breathless and angry, Tena crowded the not-so-playful Rowdy into a corner, where he couldn't keep yanking her around.

"Down! Sit!" she commanded, pressing finger-tips into his spine just where his tail joined his body. Finally the haunches sank as she increased the pressure on the nerves. "Down!" she ordered, shifting her grip on the collar so she could press on his shoulders. He growled at her. "Cut it out," she murmured, trembling inwardly as she realized there just might come a moment of truth. It happened with all pets. A moment of challenge, even from the most beloved pet, even one that wasn't a stranger but that had been raised from puppy, from kitten, from gangly-legged foal—a moment when a pet challenged authority, and that moment decided who would be boss from then on, the human or the animal. If that moment came with Rowdy, could she face it and win?

For this interval, he obeyed, much to her relief. Perhaps it was just the newness of gentle handling—somewhat gentle, anyway—and a voice that didn't shrill and hurt his ears. She patted him. He grabbed her hand in his jaws again. Carefully, with her free hand, she finger-combed his hair so she could look him right in the eye.

"No," she said calmly, gently tugging at her hand. He hung on and growled. She slid her other hand under his jaw. Rowdy growled deeply, and she felt the teeth begin to dig into her soft flesh. Suddenly she imitated Mike Mac-Gruder. "Leggo, mutt!"

Rowdy wasn't fooled. He just looked up at her with a sardonic gleam in his eyes. If he thought she was going to crouch here for hours, waiting for his owners to come home and set her free. . . .

But she didn't feel ready for a test—not yet.

"Look, Rowdy," she said uneasily, "if you want me to be nice to you, you'd better start behaving like a gentleman—because if you don't, I won't give you any *bones* or—"

Rowdy released her hand, bounded up with a bark, and dashed for the kitchen. Tena straightened slowly, ashamed of herself. She hadn't met the test. She had tricked him, fooled him but not herself. And maybe she'd been fooling herself, too—but not Mel's father—about her motives in wanting to become a veterinary. Could that be? she wondered, her face flushing crimson.

Rowdy came racing from the kitchen, skidded

on a throw rug, knocked against her, and nearly threw her off her feet. Tena followed him through the house, slowly and contritely. She shouldn't have tricked him. In the kitchen, she made him lie down again, this time careful not to let him catch her hand.

"Stay," she warned as she slowly opened the refrigerator. Rowdy bobbed to his feet and thrust his nose into the box. Pulling him back, she slammed the door. "Down! Down, I said! Now, stay! Stay!"

Twice more they went through the routine, until Rowdy got the idea that the refrigerator wasn't going to be opened until he obeyed. The big dog finally stayed on the linoleum, haunches hunched, forefeet planted firmly, ears cocked, mouth drooling, and tail whipping back and forth frenetically.

Tena saw the bottles of pop among other bottled stuff. Rowdy first, she thought. Reward him for obeying. Now, where were the beef bones she was positive Mrs. MacGruder had mentioned amid the pandemonium? There they were, in waxed paper, back of a platter of chicken. As she pulled out the package, it snagged a projecting stiff wing of chicken. The partially consumed chicken carcass tumbled from the platter to the floor. Rowdy pounced on it.

Tena whipped around. "Rowdy, no! Stay!" He spun away from her, with claws skidding on the linoleum. She grabbed and caught his tail. He doubled around, snarling past the chicken gripped in his jaws. His sudden whirling tugged her off-balance. As she went down, she would have seized him with her other hand, but it was encumbered with the package of beef bones. She lost her hold on Rowdy's tail but scrambled up quickly.

Rowdy took off through the house, with Tena in pursuit, and into the dining room, where he evidently planned to settle, with the poultry bones, under the table. She dived under after him. Growling, he retreated to the living room and squeezed behind the settee. She dragged it out from the wall.

"Rowdy, stay!"

Resignedly but determinedly, he trotted toward the stairs. Just as resignedly, and determined not to give him a chance to gnaw on chicken bones, Tena was right after him. Rowdy sped up the stairs. Tena dashed up, too—into a

bedroom, through a dressing alcove, into a bathroom, back to the hall, into another bedroom. Tena closed the door behind her to prevent his escape. Rowdy, despite his bulk, took refuge under the bed. Tena got down on hands and knees to peer under it.

"Rowdy!"

There was no mistaking the gleam of the eyes or the warning of the growl this time. She heard a crunch of chicken bone and realized that it could be her hand, even her throat, if she went under after him.

Crouching and trembling, she told herself that if the MacGruders didn't teach their dog to obey, how could they expect her to take on this responsibility? But she had seen what she was up against when she'd arrived, so shouldn't she have refused it then? She hadn't. And the same would apply if she ever became a veterinarian. If she took on the case of a sick or injured animal, she would be duty-bound to see it through. She hadn't seen it through when she'd tricked Rowdy into releasing her hand. *I didn't see it through with Mel and his father, either,* she thought. *I took the easy, indignant, and impatient way out, instead of facing them squarely and making them see where they were wrong about me.*

Tena took a deep, and what she hoped was a courageous, breath. Then, taking a pillow with her to use as a buffer, just in case, she began squirming under the bed. Rowdy growled deeply.

"Stay," she said. "It's not going to work this time, and you know it."

I hope you do, she added to herself.

She forced herself farther under the bed. Rowdy hunkered away, with another growl. Tena moved slowly, blocking his escape. He watched her with glinting eyes and a rumbling like distant thunder in his throat. Tena grabbed fast, but not for his head and the crushed chicken carcass. Instead, she clamped her hand on a rear paw and tugged hard. With a startled snarl, Rowdy let go of the chicken and coiled his body to bring his jaws toward her hand. Tena shoved the pillow into his face, got herself out from under the bed, and then dragged him out. Backing rapidly around the bedroom, pulling and lifting him with all her strength, she prevented his head from coming around at her. Finally she got hold of the other rear paw. She was too small to hold all Rowdy's weight up for long, and her arms were getting tired.

She stepped up onto the bed. It was easier on her arms to hold him that way, despite his frantic struggle to find some purchase and to get his head up.

"Quiet!" she commanded with breathless calm. "I can hold out longer than you now, Rowdy. And we're going to hold out until you discover who's boss."

It took a long time before the challenging struggle began to turn. The growls and snarls became a little less defiant; the pawing of the forefeet weakened considerably. Helpless panic began to possess the big dog. The whites of his eyes showed as he peered back and up at Tena.

"Easy, now, Rowdy," she said. "I don't want to break your spirit. Don't spoil it, Rowdy."

As she started to lower him, he began to struggle again. She lifted him once more. Before she again lowered him, she made certain that there was another pillow within quick reach. Then she released him. Rowdy quickly got all feet under him, jumped to the middle of the room, and faced around. Tena, glancing out of the corner of her eye at the pillow, resisted the temptation to grab it. Stepping slowly down from the bed, talking calmly, she moved toward the big dog. As she slowly but firmly extended her hand, he growled.

"Cut it out, Rowdy. We've reached an understanding, and you'd as well admit it."

She slapped him lightly on the side of the head as he growled again. He could have bitten her hand, but he didn't. She just kept meeting his gaze and flicking him with her fingers when she heard a faint rumble in his throat. Then she stroked his jaw gently. A pink tongue came out and tentatively licked her fingers.

"Oh, thanks, you beautiful mutt."

Tena hugged the big dog. She opened the door. He was going to surge out.

"Uh-uh!" she said sharply, pointing. "Stay! Ladies first." In the hall she said, "All right. Come!"

He bounded out joyously, then raced down the stairs. Too late, she recalled the open refrigerator and the package of beef bones on the floor. Oh, no, not again!

"Rowdy! Stay!"

He didn't come, maybe because she hurried down so fast. She found the big dog in the kitchen, eagerly sniffing the package of bones.

"Stay," she reminded him. He sat, with the package between his paws. He made no attempt to pick it up. "Good boy, Rowdy."

She spread a newspaper on the floor; then she opened the package and selected a bone. Rowdy wanted to seize it, but her voice held him back. Finally she allowed him to take it, with what he thought was gentleness.

Tena went quietly upstairs to retrieve the mangled chicken and straighten up the bedroom.

Now there was something else she must face —Mel and his father, perhaps tomorrow. She was beginning to realize that she had probably jumped to conclusions about them. Mel's father had probably been joking, or testing her, in suggesting that she'd been chasing Mel. If anything, it had been nicely the other way around, and he was undoubtedly aware of it. And as far as the scholarship went, how could he possibly have anything to do with it? Knowing her, perhaps as a future member of his family, he would certainly be accused of favoritism if he passed any kind of judgment on her application.

So maybe there was still a chance for it—on

her own merits—and money she could earn dog-sitting would be just so much extra.

There was one other thing to be faced up to: the chicken. Maybe the MacGruders wouldn't be exactly overjoyed when she told them that instead of eating doughnuts, she'd eaten their chicken and tossed the remains in the garbage.

Well, she laughed to herself, she'd just have to let them think what they would.

"But you and I will know," she said to Rowdy, who was resting his head against her knee as she watched TV, "that I didn't eat the chicken. But tomorrow I just may be eating a little crow." She laughed again. "You know something else, Rowdy? When I become a vet, I think I'm not going to have anything to do with birds or other fowl."

Rowdy looked up at her and happily let his tongue hang out. Tena parted his hair so she could look squarely at his eyes. She was positive she saw a twinkle in them.

Fly Free

Carol S. Adler

CLARE COULD FEEL the shadows surrounding her
as she sat at the desk working over her history
notes. She felt ill at ease here in the study while
members of the family passed back and forth
from kitchen to living room. If only the guest
room weren't so small! She would much rather
work there, in privacy. Not that she was ungrate-
ful; she knew they'd been generous to take her
in at all. But she could relax only when she was
alone, ever since the accident—ever since she'd
awakened in the hospital, with the bandage
covering her left hand. Now the hand with the
two missing middle fingers scurried to her lap
as she sensed Jon's presence.

"Busy?" he asked.

"I'm studying."

"So what else is new? You'll blow a fuse at the rate you're going." He sat down on the edge of the study desk, obviously preparing to tease her again.

Why didn't he give up? *I hate your clowning*, she should tell him. *I hate your incessant teasing and your lopsided smile.* Jon's mother had had enough sense to let her alone, after the first few rebuffs. His father seemed actually to *approve* of her, maybe because she was quiet and neat and stayed out of the way.

"I'll bet you've never seen the stars as bright as they are tonight," Jon was saying. "How about coming out and taking a look with me?"

"No, thanks."

"You know what you remind me of? You remind me of a hawk I had one summer. It was beautiful, like you, and it did its darnedest to bite my hand off whenever I went to feed it."

"You should have turned it loose," she said pointedly.

"It had a busted wing."

Involuntarily, her right hand moved to cover the left. "And did it heal?"

"Prettiest sight I ever saw was that bird flying off free."

"I'm not a hawk," she said, after a pause.

"No."

And my hand can't heal! she thought bitterly and wished again she could force herself to be rude to him. She turned back to her notes, but he didn't budge.

"Who're you inviting to the Drag Dance?" he asked.

"No one."

"They'll think you're stuck-up if you don't go. You haven't exactly put yourself out to be friendly at school."

"I don't care what anyone thinks."

"People who don't care what other people think don't go around trying to hide. I'd like to see you go to that Drag Dance, Clare."

"Why?"

"Just because. Matter of fact, I think I'll make it Project Number One. Be warned—you're going to that dance!" He slapped the desk masterfully and marched off on his great stork legs, exaggerating his martial stride, clowning again.

He's ridiculous, she thought, with his mischievous eyes and that grin that looked so natural on his face that it seemed to be there even when it wasn't. If he wanted a challenge, he ought to concentrate on his physics and math books. His father had already made him cut out basketball to give him more time to study. But it wasn't her business what he did. He meant nothing to her. He was just the son of friends of her mother, on whom she had been dumped for a year.

She thought angrily of the letter she hadn't been supposed to see. "I have tried everything, but Clare can't be reached. We thought perhaps a new environment, where people didn't know her before the accident. . . ." What had her mother done, except to escape from the house into her job, as always?

Her father had been kind, but he didn't understand at all. He couldn't see how hideous it made her.

"After all," he had said, "it's lucky it's your left hand. You still have the thumb and index finger to pick things up with. It'll just take a little getting used to. After a while you won't even notice it." As if she could avoid noticing when strangers, and even friends, stared! Or, if they didn't stare, they pitied, and that was worse.

She'd always been independent. She didn't need anyone now.

Tuesday afternoon Jon strode into the backyard with three other boys. Immediately she left the kitchen, where they were sure to congregate, and made for the guest room. He confronted her in the study. "Look at you," he said. "You could pose for a ghost, a beautiful, dark-eyed one, but even so, you'd better put on some lipstick. You don't want to scare them away."

"What are you talking about?" she snapped.

"I have three prospective escorts for the Drag Dance waiting for you on the patio."

"No."

"How do you know till you've met them?"

"I'm not going to be made a fool of." She turned away, her hand hidden in a fold of her skirt, but he stepped in front of her.

"Immovable object, watch out! Here comes an irresistible force." He lunged at her and had her over his shoulder before she could think. She screamed and struggled, but his mother was out shopping, and she couldn't hit him hard enough to make him let her go. He dropped her onto the chaise longue on the patio and kept her there by sitting on her.

"Comfortable?" he asked her impishly. "Tsk, tsk, tsk! Will you look at those eyes blaze? A regular conflagration going on there."

She wouldn't give him the satisfaction of saying a word. In fact, she'd never say a word to him again.

"Now that we're all here, introductions are in order," Jon said. "This handsome guy behind me is Tony Frascati. He's okay, but he's kind of stuck on himself."

"Hey, pal—some character reference you'd make!" Tony protested.

"The beefy guy chinning himself on the swing set over there is Butch. He's for you, if you like to talk sports." Jon pointed to the right. "The one staring at you in total fascination is Wayne Nelson. If you like, he'll quote poetry to you all day long."

"If you don't want to go to the dance, Clare," Wayne said eagerly, "we could take in a movie instead."

"No, thank you," she answered.

"The lady says no too easily," Jon said. "Tell you what—if you're too shy to pick one, we could have an elimination contest. Archery, maybe, or they could race. . . ."

"If you don't get off me this instant, I'll scream loud enough for the whole neighborhood to hear!" Clare said, forgetting her promise not to talk to him.

"Hey," Butch yelled, "look at me!" He balanced, feet up and head down, on the iron swing frame.

"See what powers you have, woman? He's been trying to do that for *months!*" Cautiously Jon got off her stomach but kept hold of her wrists.

"You're either a fool or a sadist, Jon Anders, and, either way, I hate you," Clare said venomously, between clenched teeth.

For an instant the smile on his face gave way to hurt.

He let go of her wrists. Immediately the good hand caught her maimed one, and she fled indoors.

"So much for that experiment," she heard Wayne say.

"See you in school," Frascati said, and she heard the sound of retreating feet.

In her room, she closed her eyes and buried her hot cheeks in the pillow. Why couldn't they let her be?

"The trouble with you," Jon said to her that evening, "is that you're an egotist. You think that what's important to you has to be important to everybody else. You're looking at a grain of sand and missing the sunset. Get what I mean?" He munched on an apple, cracking away and swallowing audibly. "Everybody has problems," he went on. "Everybody's got something he wants to hide."

"Jon!" Her voice came low and pleading. "Please leave me alone."

"My philosophizing doesn't impress you?"

"No," she said, her eyes traveling down to her left hand.

"You don't go around demanding that other people be perfect, do you? You overlook all kinds of flaws. Well, why can't you ignore one little flaw in yourself?"

She forced herself to continue her homework, pretending not to listen. His enthusiasm for the sound of his own wisdom restrained any reply she might have. "I guess the only one I'm impressing is me," he said finally. "Okay, I'll leave you to your miseries. But, Clare, you know something? Your hand's not half the problem your self-pity is."

Fly Free

That bothered her, but looking at her behavior as objectively as she could, she couldn't find much that smacked of self-pity. She neither wept for herself nor wanted others to weep. She only asked to be left alone.

That night at dinner, Jon's father acted strangely. Usually Mr. Anders said little, content to leave the burden of the conversation to his wife and son, but tonight he talked, with a false, hearty air that disconcerted Clare.

"Picked up a little present for you, Jon," he said while Clare helped Mrs. Anders clear away the soup bowls. "It's in my briefcase. Why don't you get it out now?"

Jon got up with a foolish grin on his face and went off to the living room. In a minute he was back with a framed poem, a moralistic old hammer-rhythm poem Clare remembered from elementary school days, about how if you try hard enough you can do anything.

"I see you had no trouble finding it," Mr. Anders said.

"It was the only thing in your briefcase that wasn't covered with formulas," Jon said.

"I want you to hang that over your desk. Read it every night before you sit down to study."

"Okay," Jon said. "Thanks." He sat down to his dinner again, refusing to meet the challenge in his father's eyes. Was he afraid? Clare wondered. He always treated his father with great respect, never biting back when Mr. Anders needled him.

Mr. Anders went on talking. "Met a couple of old-timers in the Bellair plant who remembered your granddad. They kept telling me what a great engineer he was. Said more or less the same things about me. I told them engineering was a family tradition with us. I told them my son was coming along soon. They thought that was something. A solid thing to be proud of."

He had stopped eating and was watching Jon as he spoke. Now he waited for his son to comment, but Jon kept methodically putting the food in his mouth and chewing, saying nothing. Finally Mr. Anders said heartily, "Well, what's the good word? Things going better with math and physics, Jon?"

"About the same," Jon said.

"Not better? With the time you have now, since you dropped sports, aren't your grades improving?"

"Not in math and physics."

64

"You're not applying yourself. You're not even trying!"

"Let me ask you something, Dad. If I didn't have any legs, would you want me to try to be a long-distance runner?"

"One year of engineering in college, and then you can switch if you still don't like it. That's fair enough, isn't it?"

"One year of engineering and I won't be able to switch. I'll have flunked out—assuming I get in, in the first place."

Mr. Anders's face reddened deeply, and a vein began to throb in his forehead. "You do well in other subjects. What's so different about these? You're just holding back on me, that's all! I want to see your recent work—tests, notes, whatever you've got. Bring it here," he bellowed. "Clare, you're in his classes. Let me see your work, too."

Brought suddenly from the audience to center stage, she felt threatened. Besides, the very idea of having her work compared to Jon's was distasteful to her. Using her good grades to wound him was foul play.

"You have nothing to be ashamed of, have you, Clare?" Mr. Anders asked.

"I'd rather not . . ." she began and petered out, unable to phrase a denial that wouldn't sound rude to her host.

"It's all right, Clare," Jon said tiredly.

Mr. Anders pushed his coffee cup aside. They laid their notebooks on the table before him. Clare felt as if she'd been shoved back into childhood, but she couldn't bring herself to protest. There was a flush on Jon's cheeks, and his smile seemed feeble. Mr. Anders immediately picked out the physics tests that had come back that day. Jon's was branded with a fat red D, Clare's with an A. A look of such rage crossed his face that Clare quailed, but Jon stood impassive. Mr. Anders didn't speak until he had control of himself again.

"Are you interested in science, Clare?"

"Not especially."

"Yet you managed to get an A. Would you say you're a great deal brighter than my son?"

"No," she said with determination, "I'm not."

"Just that you study harder, right? Would you say he prepared for this test as much as you did?"

"I don't know."

"I could have studied all night for that test, Dad, and I wouldn't have done any better. Clare has more talent for science and math than I have."

"Nonsense! She works, and you don't. You're lazy and careless."

Jon pressed on. "If I can't grab hold of high school physics, how can I expect to pass it in college?"

"You'll never get to college at the rate you're going."

"Not to an engineering school, no," he said quietly.

"It will be an engineering school or none! Get that through your head, and buckle down to the books! In fact, as of now, and until these marks start improving, you stay home weekends. If you won't work, you're not going to play, either."

Mrs. Anders spoke up then, "Arthur, his other marks are so good, don't you think it may be lack of aptitude for this sort of thing?" His mother rarely interfered. Clare was relieved to find her on Jon's side.

"It isn't a matter of can or can't! He just won't. Clare's the proof. I wish to God I'd had a child like her!" Mr. Anders stomped from the room, transformed from mild man to demon.

"Go on and do your homework, children," Mrs.

Anders said. "I'd just as soon do the dishes myself tonight."

Clare looked at Jon's face. Even though she'd only been a witness, not the victim, of Mr. Anders's onslaught, she was still shaking. But Jon didn't even look rattled, except, as he picked up the framed poem and left the room, his expression was so sad that Clare's heart turned over with sympathy for him.

When she sat down to work, she couldn't concentrate. Impulsively she stole up the stairs to the attic room, which was Jon's and which she'd never approached before. She saw him standing at the window in the dark, looking up at the stars. As soon as she said his name, he moved from the window and turned on a lamp.

"Hey," he said. "What brings you into alien territory? Aren't you afraid you'll meet a bear or something?"

His teasing cooled the tears in her eyes and almost made her sorry she had come. She stood her ground, however, and said, "Jon, I'm sorry. I didn't want your father to compare my work with yours. I wish I had been clever enough to think of a way to stop him. I'm sorry I didn't. . . ."

"You don't have to apologize. I could see you

weren't exactly crowing about being held up as an example to me."

"He had no right to attack you in front of a stranger."

"You're only a stranger in your own eyes, Clare. And about my father—you have to understand. He's been great all my life. He's done all the right things—taken me fishing and put in his bit with Little League and Scouts. He's helped me whenever I needed help. He just has this one hangup. Believe me, if I had it in me, I'd be an engineer. I'd like more than anything to make my father proud of me."

His attitude surprised her so that she couldn't speak at once. Then she burst out, "But he's so unreasonable about it! Couldn't your mother talk to him, or maybe the guidance counselor at school?"

"They've tried. Look, one of these days I'll be doing so well at something—I don't know what yet, but something—that he'll come round. He's not dense. It will get through to him someday that there are other things in the world besides engineering. It'll just take time and patience, that's all."

Clare stared at him a second, then she nodded.

"Yes, of course, you're right." She left without telling him what she was thinking, though all through the next week, she tried by her attitude to show him how much she thought of him. She smiled when their paths crossed in school, and she accepted his kitchen banter and returned it to him as best she could, considering her natural seriousness.

Once he said to her, "You've changed. You're relaxed now. I like that." But he looked puzzled, as if he didn't quite understand what had changed her.

She *wanted* him to know. She wanted to make amends. But she didn't get a chance to really talk to him until Saturday night, the night of the Drag Dance he had wanted her to attend. His parents were out. Jon had gone obediently upstairs to "hit the old physics book," as he put it, but in half an hour he was out in the kitchen rattling pans. The smell of burning grease made Clare put down the novel she was reading and go into the kitchen to investigate. He stood at the range, frantically agitating a panful of smoking fat and unpopped popcorn.

"Get the physics book and find out why this stuff's not popping," Jon quipped. The black smoke tickled the ceiling as Clare took the pan and poured the mess down the disposal.

"That's an insulting way to treat my culinary efforts," he complained.

"Popcorn making, like any other task, is simple if you know how," she said. "Observe!" She washed and dried the pan, with her right hand doing the work and her left unobtrusively holding the handle, got out a measuring cup, and poured in some salad oil. Jon watched obediently. When the oil was hot, she added a third of a cup of popcorn, clamped a lid on the pan, and shook it gently.

In a few minutes she had a panful of bright white bubbles of corn. Jon got out the salt, sat down at the kitchen table, and said, "Outstanding dunderhead of the year is what they ought to crown me. To flunk physics, okay, but not even to pop corn right—boy, I don't know!"

"You're anything but a dunderhead," she said so soberly that he looked up at her. "You're the most mature person I've ever known."

"Hey," he said, "is there someone else in the room?" He pretended to look around. "Sit down and have some popcorn with me."

She sat. "You accept yourself as you are," she

71

persisted, relieved to be telling him finally. "That's part of what maturity means, isn't it? At least, that's what you've been trying to tell me."

"How about that? I always knew I had something. Good popcorn, Clare."

"I think you have a lot. I think—" she paused, embarrassed—"I think you're pretty wonderful."

He looked at her, for once at a loss for words. Then, "What this party needs is some music." He got up and switched on the radio, tuning in a slow dance tune. "I said I'd get you to dance tonight." He held out his arms to her. "Let's dance."

At once she tensed. Her left hand curled shut and hid against her waist. He waited patiently, with his arms extended in invitation while she hesitated. Then her fingers unbent. She thrust both hands into his in a gesture of trust. He pulled her to her feet, and they began to move together to the music. There were no decorations, no live band, Clare thought dreamily, but even a little square of kitchen has atmosphere when the mood is right.

A Person, After All

Constance Kwolek

HOW ABOUT THAT?" said Anne Morgan's brother at the breakfast table. "Guess who died."

"Somebody I know?" She put down her cereal spoon and extended her hand for the newspaper. Normie held it out to her teasingly but did not release it.

They sat like this for several seconds, her brother's eyes mischievous behind the tortoise-shell rim of his glasses. Shadows of hand and newspaper pages, then hand again, fell across the sunny tabletop and lay there.

"Ah, it doesn't matter," Anne said, a trifle annoyed. She picked up her spoon again and tipped her cereal bowl. The last drops of sugary milk lay in a spoon-sized pool for her to finish.

"Just Old Starkley, that's who," her brother said, bored now. He rose from the table and collected his homework and a science book from the kitchen counter.

"Old Starkley?" A stab of surprise went through her. It was as if bone marrow had shivered, then settled, solid again.

Old Starkley was not really old. Dull, maybe, lacking enthusiasm, unable to join in with the exuberance of her pupils. *Dull* Starkley. . . .

"You're kidding," Anne said.

"Nope," Normie told her. He went out the screen door, letting it slam behind him. Anne reached over to the counter for the Millington *Gazette* and opened it to the obituary page.

She sat alone and looked at the boldface columns tightly packed with words, facts, statistics. Name after name—total strangers—and the one significant square, outlining a person she knew—had known—Old Starkley.

Miss Starkley. Suddenly. (Of course, sudden. She had been at the front of her classroom yesterday, as usual, pinch-faced and punitive.) Names of relatives. Funeral home. Church. Place of interment.

Neatly packed into a few inches of newsprint, this was Old Starkley, who had Maintained Order, who had evoked some respect, some scorn, even some secret merriment from her English classes, until and including yesterday afternoon.

There was a slim column and a broad headline missing from page one, where Normie had neatly scissored out an item for Current Events. The pages rustled like taffeta as Anne riffled through them.

First page, second section, important news of local interest:

> MISS SARA STARKLEY, MILLINGTON EDU-
> CATOR, FATALLY STRICKEN AT FUND-
> RAISING DANCE.

At a *dance. Old Starkley?*

But why not? Anne remembered something now. As freshmen, she and her friends had not yet set their teachers into molds, into private niches based on this student's rumor and that student's complaint.

Therefore they had found nothing unusual about Miss Starkley, standing in the chaperons' corner with a dark-haired, pleasant-faced man.

The two of them danced several times. He spoke to her with attentiveness and got her a paper cup of cola as they looked on at the young people assembled in the gymnasium.

Later, that night was forgotten, overshadowed by student lore: Old Starkley's clothes, just the wrong side of stylish, and that face, so at odds with her spare white arms and legs.

Old Starkley's face was creased and ruddy. When a girl from one of her classes showed up with an old rich brown chamois purse, the secretly whispered taunt was born: Old Starkley had a chamois face.

Miss Sara Rosamund Starkley, 32—thirty-two? Younger even than Mother and Dad, and they weren't old. Then why. . . . Because Sara Starkley was humorless. Unlike Mr. Jennings, for instance, who had a bubbling penchant for shrewd, illuminating puns, Miss Starkley never thought anything was funny.

Unlike some of the other teachers, she was never able to lower her guard, to be less remote, to reach her students. There seemed to be a pane of glass at the front of the English classroom, with Old Starkley on the stern and lonely side of the invisible barrier.

Once, just once, this pane of glass had shattered. The class was analyzing *Macbeth* one afternoon, and Miss Starkley had grown excited.

"Can you imagine what a perceptive man Shakespeare was? To have that woman feel such guilt, such dreadful guilt, and the compulsion, the obsession, that the blood was still there! You see, boys and girls, it is authentic; it is accurate, even by today's standards. William Shakespeare knew intuitively all about modern psychology, that long ago. . . ."

She had paced the wooden floor near the blackboard, wringing her pale hands. That chamois face was radiant as she lost herself in Lady Macbeth's anguish: "Out, damned spot! Out, I say!"

After an initial delighted surprise that hushed the class, they had not been allowed to react. She suddenly unclasped her narrow hands and lowered her eyes to the textbook, dryly resuming the discussion. The barrier rose again between teacher and class, like a flower closing.

Daughter of Mrs. Adam Twyning of this city and Michael Starkley of Los Angeles, California. Then there must have been a divorce. Anne knew a girl whose parents had gotten a divorce.

"Annie, do you suppose I did it? I feel as if it's my fault. I made them get the divorce, didn't I? Do you think it's all my fault?"

The face of Anne's friend became, in her mind's eye, the face of Miss Starkley, a deep worry crease at the bridge of her nose, her lips pinched, her eyes full of trembling, forestalling tears.

. . . and the sister of Adam Twyning, Jr., prominent Millington athlete. So she'd had a half-brother, much younger, more accomplished.

This, then, might have been a meeting point for Anne and her teacher, had Old Starkley ever become a real person to her. (I have a much younger brother, too, Miss Starkley. . . .)

Anne seldom mentioned, even to her friends, how unhappy it sometimes made her to think that she had to slave for every passing mark, while Normie, in sixth grade, seemed to grasp the most difficult words, theories, ideas, with total ease.

. . . poetry prizes in college. . . .

So she had had dreams, like everyone else.

Miss Starkley was stricken at a square dance held by the Over-Twenty-One Ski Club, a benefit for the Millington Children's Home, of which

*she was a committee member and a volunteer
worker.*

Images moved rapidly through Anne's mind,
pictures having nothing to do with a chamois-
faced, stern English teacher.

Old Starkley . . . no, Sara Rosamund Starkley,
trim in ski pants and a gay parka . . . Sara in a
happy snowball fight, maybe with the man
who'd been her escort at the Freshman Frolic
. . . Sara on a ski slope . . . sun and snow and
wind rushing at her. This was why the weath-
ered chamois-colored face, the sign of Sara's
other life, away from corridors and heated
rooms smelling of sneakers, chalk dust, and
ridicule.

*. . . heart seizure . . . friends attempted to
revive her . . . Millington rescue squad . . . re-
suscitator. . . .*

Mother had come down the back stairs into
the kitchen. Her arms were full of white sheets
like huge, deflated beach balls.

"Mother? My English teacher died," Anne
said. "Last night."

"Oh? Which one was that?" She rummaged
in the cupboard for detergent and fabric
softener.

"Old . . . Miss Starkley. You know. You met her at Parents' Night."

"Did I?" Mother paused at the cellar door, bright boxes set atop the pyramid of white sheets in her arms. "Isn't that too bad. I can't seem to place her, though."

Anne opened her mouth to tell her mother, to make her remember Miss Starkley as she had suddenly begun to remember her, but the words would not come.

She heard the voices of her friends as they came around the corner of the house. Hurriedly Anne stacked the breakfast dishes in the sink. Folding the *Gazette* in half, she tossed it on the pile for the Cub Scouts' paper drive, ready to be taken away.

Gathering up her books from the counter top, she went out the door and down the steps past the lilac bush.

Miss Starkley had always used a lily-of-the-valley cologne, and Anne had never noticed it until now, in sudden remembrance. Sara Rosamund probably would have liked a bouquet of lilacs for her desk. Anne had thought of taking her such a bouquet—ah, no. Tell the truth. She had never thought of it.

"Did you hear?" "What do you think of it?" "Wonder who'll take Miss Starkley's place."

"I was so surprised to think of Miss Starkley—" Anne began. Like the other girls, she was referring to the teacher in a different, more respectful way.

They went back down the Morgans' driveway. Several boys they knew were walking by on the sidewalk. Loudly, they greeted one another. The solemn moment had passed.

"Can you picture Old Starkley square dancing? I can't."

Tentative giggles grew into general, more familiar, laughter.

Anne felt sudden anger. Then, just as suddenly, she felt nothing.

For a moment she had wanted to shout at them, to tell them that Miss Sara Rosamund Starkley had had a life outside the classroom— that she had been a real person, after all. Anne wanted to tell them about the vivid images she had of events in the teacher's life, to which none of them had ever been a witness.

But they wouldn't understand, even if she were to tell them. They would have to learn for themselves how to read between the lines.

Two Nice Girls

Frances Gray Patton

VESTA BETHEA and Sally B. Boatwright were careful not to look at each other as they left the meeting at Canterbury House, the Episcopal Student Center at Kenan University; they were afraid they would burst out laughing if they did. Vesta could feel tears of mirth swimming over her eyes, making the irises very dark and the whites very brilliant, and could only pray they would be taken for tears of dedication. Sally B., whose thin skin turned either pale or pink with her passing moods, knew her face was flushed. With the pretty manners their mothers had taught them, they said their good-byes. They were gracious to the special guests of the

82

afternoon, a group of students from a neigh-
boring college for blacks, and properly demure
to the middle-aged clergymen, their own chaplain and his visitor—though when those gentlemen beamed on them with an expression of
yearning benevolence, they had trouble keeping
their composure. However, they managed. They
went out into the warm sunlight of a Carolina
fall—two nice girls who, from a distance,
looked as alike as paper dolls cut in a chain.
They were the same height (a shade below
average) and the same build, with small waists,
modest bosoms, and rather long, slender legs.
They both wore short, full-skirted cotton dresses
and matching cardigans. They both had good
carriage—as if they valued themselves—and they
both walked so lightly that the topknots of freshman class ribbons scarcely bobbed on their
shining hair. The only apparent difference between them was that Vesta was a black girl,
dressed in yellow, and Sally B. was white,
wearing blue.

Not until they had turned off the main path
and were in a small grove of golden maples, well
removed from the Center, did the girls allow
themselves to laugh aloud. A starling, picking at

winter-grass seed just beyond the clump of trees, flew away in alarm.

"Look! We scared the poor little bird!" cried Vesta.

"Good," said Sally B. "Nasty old starling. Avaunt! *Departez-vous!* Scram!" She blew her nose on a crumpled piece of tissue. "When he said that, I nearly collapsed! I dug my nails into my palms. I told myself, 'Think about something tragic. Joan of Arc at the stake, Socrates drinking the hemlock—'"

"Grapenut ice cream for dessert," put in Vesta merrily.

The girls were laughing because they had just attended a meeting at which a most serious subject—the Christian's duty to promote racial equality—had been discussed with an earnestness that had embarrassed them, and then ("Like comic relief straight from heaven," Vesta said afterward) something funny had happened to release them from strain. They were laughing, also, because they had sensed, in a wonderful rush of feeling, a basic congeniality between themselves that made them light-headed with happiness.

They had been acquainted for more than two

months, ever since the annual Freshman Reception, and, because their surnames began with the same letter, sat side by side in a couple of big lecture courses. Moreover, as high scorers on a verbal aptitude test, they had both been placed in a select English class, where they read for honors and were encouraged to form critical opinions. They had discovered in each other many similarities of taste and temperament. They were both somewhat bookish, somewhat fastidious, and somewhat inclined to consider other people obtuse. They both liked modern poetry, satirical novels, Shakespeare's plays (except *Othello*, which they found painful), and hot tea. They thought Shelley absurd, Ibsen stuffy, and Thomas Wolfe sloppy. They eschewed YWCA get-togethers, boys who grew beards, and grapenut ice cream. Both, from choice, roomed alone. To hear girls talk about their "roomies," they said, made their flesh crawl. Yet it hadn't been until this afternoon, as they'd sat together in the back of the room, wincing whenever what they called "dean jargon" (words like "rewarding," "enriching," and "fellowship") was flung at them, that they had longed to abandon the last vestige of reserve and reveal them-

selves ruthlessly to each other. In the other's
company, each imagined she could let herself
go, clown, exaggerate, bare her soul—in short,
feel perfectly natural and perfectly charming.

"He said, 'Dat'—" Vesta began, but a fresh
fit of giggles seized her. With a white linen
handkerchief she dabbed at the tears that spilled
from her eyes.

What had set the girls off was not worthy of
such prolonged hilarity but had, in fact, been
mildly amusing. The main hall of Canterbury
House was equipped to serve both profane and
sacred purposes. At one end was a chancel, with
communion rail and altar, which could, on occa-
sions like that of today's meeting, be hidden by a
screen, so that the rest of the hall became a
secular auditorium. After the meeting had
adjourned, the chaplain, known as "Padre" to
his affectionate flock, had lifted the screen in
order to show the visiting black minister the
mural above the altar. The mural, done by a
former student, depicted in abstract terms—
great wheels and curves and upthrust fountains
of color—the Ascension from the Mount. It was
entirely incomprehensible to the visitor, who,
as soon as he recovered from his shock, had

87

declared valiantly: "That is what I call *art!*"

Vesta began again. "He said, '*Dat* is what Ah call—'"

"He didn't!" said Sally B.

"You were too nice to notice," said Vesta. "All of us are liable to talk that way when we're startled. Amos-and-Andy talk. One time I walked up behind Mama when she was sewing and thought she was alone in the house, and she hollered out, 'Who dat?' as plain as anything. But when I teased her, she swore the truth wasn't in me. She was so insulted, she wouldn't open her mouth to me for a solid hour!"

Sally B. leaned against the bole of a maple, shaking with laughter and trying to stop—for to laugh at somebody's mother was, of course, uncouth. And suddenly a flash of insight sobered her. Vesta, she realized, had not told her little tale at random. She had meant to stress the difference between them—"the accident of pigmentation," as their dear Padre had said—and to impose a condition. *If they were to be friends*, Vesta had said in effect, *they could not ignore the difference. They would have to mention it, explore it, accept it for what it was.* Vesta's move was gallant, and in the first heat of admiration,

88

Sally B. was inclined to match it. But she grew cautious. A friendship with Vesta would amount to a commitment. It could not be sloughed off, like an ordinary campus attachment, in indifference or a moment of pique. She would have to continue it for a long time, perhaps forever, even if she found it awkward. Even if—as seemed unlikely but was possible—it became a bore.

"Quit hugging that tree," said Vesta. "You'll ruin your sweater."

"It's just a cheesy little rag," Sally B. answered with a shrug.

"Well, you won't help it by treating it mean," said Vesta. She stroked the sleeve of her own sweater, which was cashmere.

Vesta was far better dressed than Sally B. or most of her other classmates. Even her cotton dress was meticulously tailored from a fabric chosen for its silkiness of texture and the shade of yellow that complemented the clear, strong brown of her complexion. She was the first black undergraduate to enter Kenan (the only one, so far, for the trustees of the university had not revised their policy of racial exclusiveness until late in the preceding spring, after most high school seniors had completed their arrangements

STILL MORE OF THE BEST

for the fall), and as soon as her application had been accepted; her mother, a dressmaker, had started assembling for her an absolutely perfect college wardrobe.

Sally B. brushed a few crumbs of bark from her blue sweater. "Come on," she said. "If we stay here whooping and hollering, we'll scare more than the birds."

"People will think we're for the birds," said Vesta.

As they left the grove for the open campus, Vesta and Sally B. made talk about the autumn leaves ("Yesterday they were pellucid," said Vesta. "But today they're brassy, like a peroxide blonde"), about their English instructor's opinion of *The Great Gatsby*, about the idiosyncrasies of their house counselors, and about what they would do in case of atomic attack. Now and then they were hailed by other co-eds. Three girls playing canasta in the sun on the library steps urged them to join the game. One group invited them to have drinks at the snack shop and another to listen to records in the lounge of the music building. Though those invitations included Sally B., they were all directed, with pointed cordiality, to Vesta.

"My! You're Miss Popularity!" Sally B. said as they paused in the middle of a dormitory quadrangle, at a spot that was normally the parting of their ways. To the right, down a flagstone walk, stood Vesta's dormitory; to the left stood its twin, Sally B.'s.

"I'm not popular," Vesta said. "I'm just everybody's conscience."

Sally B. made her decision. "If you'll come up to my little garret," she said, "I'll fix us a spot of real teapot tea that will inspire us to real conversation. I'll have to make it with hot water from the bathroom tap, but that's so hot it's scalding. At least we won't have to face those ghastly snack-shop tea bags. They remind me of little drowned animals with long tails."

"Okay," said Vesta. "I have a dinner date, but I guess there's time. I'm eating steak in the Pine Room with a medical student. He's black."

"So what?" said Sally B. "*I* wouldn't care if he was green."

"My mama and my brother P. G. would," said Vesta. "They'd skin me alive. But he's the blackest boy you ever saw!"

"I've got a date tonight, too," said Sally B., "with this old Sigma Chi from down near home.

He's not real cute, but he's white."

Sally B.'s room was under the eaves of the building. On the gray linoleum floor was a worn Persian scatter rug; the narrow bed was covered with a patchwork quilt; books and papers were strewn every which way. On the desk was a gooseneck lamp with a green celluloid shade; over it hung a print, a Picasso family group from his Blue Period. The dresser was bare, except for a silver-backed brush and comb. In the embrasure of the dormer window stood a trunk, upon which reposed a large silver tray laden with a squat-bellied brown teapot, a tin of tea, two china cups and saucers, and a few silver spoons in a silver christening mug.

"I haven't a thing to go in it or with it," said Sally B. as she took the pot and the tin from the tray. "I'm so in the habit of drinking mine straight."

"I prefer tea uncorrupted," said Vesta, who had a sweet tooth and was bitterly disappointed by the absence of sugar. "What a civilized room! I'm glad it's not cluttered with banalities—pandas and all that beddy-bye junk!"

"I like restraint," said Sally B. "And you'll notice my parents aren't sitting out, either—

staring at us from expensive frames!"

"Mine are," said Vesta. Because of her lie about the tea, she felt she mustn't avoid the truth again.

"Well, that's a matter of preference," Sally B. said quickly, reflecting that, of course, Vesta would have to display her parents' pictures for fear of seeming ashamed to. "At least you don't kiss them good night, like some creeps I know!"

"Some nights I do," said Vesta.

"I fear I'm colder than a serpent's tooth," said Sally B., who carried snapshots of her mother and father in her wallet. "I'll just zip down to the bathroom and brew our potion. Make yourself at home."

Left alone, Vesta surveyed the room, comparing it to her own, which was chintzy and spruce, like a college girl's room in *House Beautiful*. Here the rug was threadbare in places; the bedspread was homemade and faded. The silver back of the brush was dented, she noticed as she stood before the mirror to put on fresh lipstick, and the initials engraved upon it were not Sally B.'s. Everything appeared to be a hand-me-down that had suffered hard use. The Boatwrights must be hard up, Vesta thought, with a stab of pity for her new friend. She had guessed so from Sally B.'s clothes. She moved over to the window to examine the cups on the trunk. They, at least, were lovely. They were white, as thin as eggshells, with gold handles and gold rims.

Sally B. returned. "Have a seat," she said. "On the bed or the chair, whichever you'd rather. We'll have to use the floor for a table."

Vesta took the chair—a desk chair provided by the university. "This is good," she said falsely as she sipped her tea, which contained leaves and was too weak. "And your cups are out of this world."

"Thank you," said Sally B. "They were my grandmother's cups—my great-great-grand-mother's, really—but Grandma left them to me, along with the old Sheffield waiter on the trunk. The cups came from France. Look!" She held hers aloft. "The light shines through them!"

"I'm surprised they let you bring them to school," said Vesta.

"They wanted me to," said Sally B. "You see, down in Frye's Ferry, my native heath, they think any place west or north of the Cape Fear region is a land of barbarians. So when I came

up here—three hundred long miles from Culture!
—they wanted me to have things to remind me
of who I was. As my mother said when I left,
'Remember, *we* are the people who set the
standards.'"

"My mother said something like that, too,"
said Vesta. "They all do." She smiled. "But up
in Queen City—the hub of the Piedmont—"

"My father calls the Piedmont the Yankee part
of the Carolinas," said Sally B.

"I resent that, but I'll let it pass," Vesta said
affably. "Anyway, in Queen City, we think flat-
country people are living in the Dark Ages."

"And how right you are!" said Sally B. "Compared to Frye's Ferry, Queen City is really a
metropolis."

"The last census gave us ninety-seven thou-
sand," said Vesta. "With the suburbs, we're well
over a hundred."

"Our population is twenty-four hundred and
sixty-three," said Sally B., "counting the corpses
still on the registration books. But we're a county
seat, and we're right on the water, and, well, the
Boatwrights and the Fryes, my mother's folks,
sort of started the place back before the Revolu-
tion. The rest of our family's moved away, but

95

the graveyard is full of us, so it's home. 'The land of lost content,' I reckon. 'The happy highways where I went'—"

" 'And cannot come again,' " Vesta supplied.

"No. Not in my old provincial way," said Sally B. "Not now that I can view it from a perspective, with urbane eyes." She sighed. "But I brought some of it with me. That lamp on the desk—it was my grandfather's when he studied at Chapel Hill. My cups and spoons and waiter. The dilapidated rug and the quilt on my bed. I slept under that quilt from the time I was seven. Nobie, my grandmother's cook, pieced it from scraps she'd collected. I never lost any love on her, nor she on me, but she gave it to me—out of spite, I always thought, because she knew I was plaguing Mother to buy me a satin-covered eiderdown. And now I'm sentimental about it."

Sally B. gazed at the tea leaves in the bottom of her cup. Her thoughts made a half-formed vignette of Frye's Ferry, a gently decaying old Carolina town, delightfully situated at the confluence of two tidal rivers, from which progress —for some reason mysterious to its inhabitants —had drifted away. She remembered climbing from the attic, up a wobbly ladder and through

a trapdoor, to the widow's walk on the roof of
her house and seeing what she had thought was
the whole wide world spread out below: the
crowns of the live oaks, listing to leeward and
shaved flat by the wind, the clock tower of the
church, and the estuarial waters reflecting every
change in the weather or time of day—gray
clouds, blue sky, red sunset, the rising of the
moon. She thought of the big house beneath
the roof—the oil portraits crazed by time, the
crystal chandelier in the hall that tinkled whenever a door was opened and was generally
gauzed with cobwebs, and the library, the heart
of the house, where the family sat after supper
and where she had read straight through sets of
calf-bound books known as "classics," simply
because she had nothing else to read.

Outdoors, on the south chimney, was the Carolina jessamine vine, so enchantingly fragrant in
spring when it dripped with long-throated yellow blossoms that a child could stick on her
fingers for gloves. And there was her father,
inspecting his not extensive grounds with the air
of a country squire—walking stiffly because of
his artificial leg and engaging in long remi-
niscences with Caesar, the elderly yardman,

who was never sorry to have his labors interrupted. Forgetting the tawdriness of Frye's
Ferry's main street, the sultry oppression of its
summers, and the unmitigated boredom of the
bleak winters, Sally B. longed to show Vesta its
charm. But she could not find the words to
convey both affection and sophisticated detach-
ment. Besides—would Vesta be interested?

"I suppose you signed the petition Padre
passed around," said Sally B. "I did."

"Natch," said Vesta. "Not to would have been
like standing up in church and saying you didn't
care to be saved. But I didn't sign the pledge
to demonstrate tomorrow. I positively *couldn't!*"

"Neither did I," said Sally B. "But I feel like
a sissy. I believe in the principle morally, and
maybe I ought to believe emotionally."

"You can't force emotions," said Vesta.

"You can try," said Sally B. "I mean, just
because I'm a deep-dyed, seventh-generation
southerner and nobody *expects* me to protest—
maybe that's precisely why it's my duty to."

"I'm a southerner myself," said Vesta. "Seven
generations or more, and"—she grinned—"a
whole lot deeper-dyed than you are. But I'm
not about to go out to any junction of the high-

way and stand in front of any Purple Rooster Restaurant, praying and singing hymns. I've never been that hungry!"

"It's the principle that counts," said Sally B.

"I marched in a picket line once in Queen City because my Sunday School teacher preached, like you, about principles," said Vesta. "Never again! It was awful. So public. I carried a placard that said, 'We are good enough to cook here—why can't we eat here?' What sense did that make? We hire a cook at home, but she doesn't take her meals with us. Does yours?"

"My mother's our cook since old Nobie died," said Sally B. "And sometimes me. We have Caesar's wife to straighten up for us. My father says she's above suspicion—of prejudice against dust. But your picketing—did it accomplish anything?"

"Sure. The dime store desegregated its lunch counters," said Vesta. "Me—I wouldn't be caught dead eating in a dime store!"

"I'm not wild about the Purple Rooster's food," Sally B. said absently. "Their French fries are good, though."

"I hate them," said Vesta. "Most all the eating places at home are wide-open now, except the social clubs. The new motel out on the Asheville Road takes blacks overnight."

Sally B. nodded. "Our old Caesar stayed up there last year at his church convention. He told Daddy it was 'jes' as *clean!*'"

Both girls set their cups on the floor and rocked with laughter.

"My point is," said Vesta, when she regained command of herself, "that this is a legal matter. Whether the Purple Rooster has a constitutional right to arbitrarily exclude people from their place of business is for the courts to decide, not me or you or the Canterbury Fellowship of Kenan University. Not even the church. I haven't got much religion, but what I do have is private and personal and nonpolitical, strictly between me and God."

"My father says the poor parsons have stopped believing in God, and all they have left is integration," Sally B. said. She stopped short. "Oh —I'm sorry!"

"For what?" Vesta demanded. "If we aren't ruthless, we can't truly communicate."

"I'm sorry if I made my father sound like a bigot," said Sally B. "He's not. He just likes being witty."

100

"He *is* witty," said Vesta. "Witty as all get-out!"

"Don't be sarcastic," begged Sally B. "Except when he was at Chapel Hill and then in the Army during World War Two, he's spent his life right there in Frye's Ferry, in the house where he was born. So, naturally, his horizons are limited by environment."

"Dean jargon," said Vesta. "What does he do?"

"He practices some law," said Sally B. "Not very much. He lost a leg in Normandy. So he stays sort of close—supervising Caesar and reading and listening to records. And talking."

"Does your mother work?"

"No," said Sally B. "She fishes."

"She what?"

"Fishes," said Sally B. "She doesn't care for gardening or reading or cards, and she can't collect antiques, because the house is jam-packed with 'em. Our backyard goes down to the river. We have a little dock and a rowboat."

"She stays out in the boat all day?"

"Sometimes she casts from the shore," said Sally B. "In bad weather, she ties flies."

"Oh," said Vesta.

Suddenly Sally B. remembered her mother's

eyes, innocent and, with her windburned face, so blue you could hardly believe it. "She's solitary by nature—like me, I guess. I didn't mean to make fun of her."

"We're a solitary-natured family, too," said Vesta. "We keep to ourselves. I guess you could call us snobs."

Her father, Vesta said, had been dead for eight years. He had been, like his father before him, head steward at the most fashionable men's club in Queen City, a man of great presence, who bore himself as if he had royal blood in his veins—which he did have, actually, since he could trace his descent back to an African king who had been brought to America in a slave ship. (This was clearly a legend, Sally B. thought. But what Boatwright or Frye dared to smile at a family legend?)

Because of his superiority, Vesta explained, he had been placed in command of a rice plantation—a kind of island kingdom populated entirely by blacks. He had been an absolute monarch, with power of life and death over his subjects. "When he stalked through the fields—he was seven feet tall—they all bowed down and rubbed their foreheads in the dirt. If they didn't, he

102

had them barbecued for dinner!" As Vesta went on, expanding in gruesome detail upon the savage glories of her progenitor, her face assumed (or so Sally B. felt) an alien, primitive beauty that was dazzling and a trifle eerie. Her skin glowed like the surface of a walnut table rubbed hard with wax. Her eyes glittered. Between her parted red lips—not thick, exactly, but full enough to be Negroid—her teeth looked extraordinarily white and sharp. Then she laughed, and her face became a Vesta face again, quiet and heart-shaped.

"I blew it up a bit for your benefit," she said. "You looked so scared, I couldn't help myself."

"Tell me more," said Sally B.

There was little more to tell, Vesta said. The owners of the royal slave had christened him Prince George, though the "George" was a puzzle—a Charles must have been reigning in England at the time. At any rate, the name had been preserved in the family. It was passed down to the firstborn male in each succeeding generation.

"Like the Sons of the Cincinnati," Sally B. interpolated. "Daddy's one."

"It was Papa's name," said Vesta. "My brother

103

has it now. He was called Prince, for short, till some white boys at a golf course where he caddied told him it was a dog's name. They whistled at him: 'Here, Prince! Here, Prince!'"

"How cruel!" gasped Sally B.

. "They were nothing but trash," Vesta shrugged. "It was a municipal course, where any tack with fifty cents could play. But after that he called himself P. G."

Her mother, Vesta said, came from an orphanage. No one knew whose child she was, but you could tell from her delicate bones that she was "quality." In her teens she had been a nursemaid in the house of an Episcopal rector. There she had discovered her talent for sewing—first making doll clothes for the little children and later helping the rector's wife with party dresses for the older girls. After marriage to Prince George Bethea, she had started taking in sewing for the best families in Queen City. Now she had a flourishing business, with three seamstresses working under her.

"She's more a couturiere than a dressmaker," Vesta said. "She specializes in trousseaux and debutante gowns."

"Lucky you!" said Sally B. "My mother can't

sew on a button without its falling right off."
She scowled. "I suppose I'll have to be presented
at the Governor's Christmas Ball, and I'll look
like an ad for a rummage sale!"

"I might be able to help you," Vesta said.
"Sometimes the post-debs bring their gowns
back to Mama, to sell at half price."

"That's an idea," Sally B. said vaguely. "I don't
know, though. I may pass the whole thing up.
Debuts are anachronistic."

"We have this big old gingerbready house
across the street from the bus station," said
Vesta. "Authentic Charles Addams. Mama and
Papa bought it for a song when the neighborhood was rezoned. It gave Mama space for her
fitting rooms. But with Papa passed away and
P. G. gone most of the time—he got his A.B. at
Howard, and now he's at Harvard Law—Mama
and I rattle around in it, and it's a little bit lonesome. We have no neighbors except a Chinese
laundry and a used-car lot." She had attended
an all-black high school, Vesta continued, but
had been discouraged from forming close friend-
ships there. Her mother had driven her to school
each morning and had come for her "smack on
the dot of three twenty-five" each afternoon.

105

"Some of the kids were awfully nice but not nice enough for Mama."

"I'm an only child," said Sally B. "I rode to the county school on the school bus, and then I rode home again. That was that. I went to Wilmington once a month to stay with my cousins and let the dentist fiddle with my braces. In summer I went to the beach for a while. But there was literally nobody my age to associate with in Frye's Ferry."

"I considered going to Central High," said Vesta. "Queen City has token school integration. But Mama said that was silly. Most aristocratic white girls at home go off to boarding school, and she didn't want me exposed to the tolerance of the riffraff. I guess that's why I have a horror of the Purple Rooster mess. There'll be press photographers, and I might appear in the newspapers—or even on national TV—trying to crash into a lower-middle-class place where I'm not wanted!"

"I can see how you feel," said Sally B.

"I didn't petition to enter Kenan," Vesta said. "I was invited to apply."

"I know," said Sally B. It was common knowledge that the Kenan Alumni Club of Queen City had chosen Vesta ("a girl with white instincts") to be the first representative of her race at the university.

"They offered me a scholarship, but I refused it," said Vesta. "Mama didn't want me to be beholden."

"*I'm* sure beholden—and glad to be!" said Sally B. "Without a grant-in-aid, I couldn't have come here!"

"It's a wonderful school," said Vesta. "People have been awfully nice to me. And if anyone ever showed me contempt, I wouldn't be shattered. I'd show it right back."

"Spit in their eye," said Sally B.

"But I don't go hunting for insults, feeling injured if some girl with a lot on her mind doesn't smile when she says hello or imagining that anybody who whispers to anybody else is whispering about me," Vesta said. "I take it as a sign of gentility never to question a motive. In other words, life's not a novel by Henry James."

"Golly, that's good!" Sally B. exclaimed. "Mind if I use it?"

"It's not original," Vesta confessed. "One of P. G.'s professors said it in a lecture. I haven't read any James but *The Turn of the Screw*."

"Me either," said Sally B. "That governess—"

They plunged into a discussion of abnormal psychology, which led, as night to day, to sex.

"I'm as ignorant as a new-laid egg," said Vesta. "I've gleaned a few facts of life from books and from hanging around Mama's fitting rooms. Mama says women in their underthings will tell anything. But as for personal experience—why, I've practically never been alone with a boy!"

"I've done a little light necking at the beach," said Sally B., blushing. "Nothing serious. Just enough to get a notion of what the fuss is all about." She gave Vesta an owl-eyed look. "And it's my uneducated guess that the real thing—when you're terrifically in love, I mean—must be utterly divine! Why else are all the lady deans so afraid we'll take the plunge every time we get a chance?"

"This date I have tonight, though," Vesta said nervously. "I've barely met him. I've heard med students have their own ideas about women."

"Athletes are the worst," said Sally B., "when they break training."

"Is your Sigma Chi an athlete?"

"*Him?*" said Sally B. scornfully. "He gets winded watching bowling on television!"

108

Sex led to ethics, and ethics to religion.

"Like you, I'm not a hard believer," said Sally B. "Sometimes I feel hypocritical when I say the Apostles' Creed. But I talked to our rector in Frye's Ferry—he happens to be my cousin, Cooper Trent—and he told me not to worry, that all intelligent people have doubts. He said the important thing—the essence of the Christian attitude—was contained in one verse of the Litany. 'From hardness of heart, good Lord, deliver us.' "

"I'll buy that," said Vesta. "Religion is a private affair. Mass production vulgarizes it!"

"Hardness of heart!" Sally B. said softly, as if she hadn't heard Vesta. "That would be a terrible sickness to have!"

"You needn't fear it, Sally B.," said Vesta.

"I hope not," said Sally B. "But I'm aloof, you know. I don't consider all men my brothers."

"Who does?" asked Vesta.

"There's this old gentleman," said Sally B. "A retired professor, I think, with this mangy beard, who comes to the library—"

"He haunts it," said Vesta. "He's the library ghost."

"He sat beside me at a table in the reading

109

room this morning," said Sally B. "He has hairs growing out of his ears, and his lip hangs down like a horse's. You can hear him breathe! I thought, what would I do if he fell off his chair with a stroke or something and I had to touch him?"

"Ugh!"

"Then it came to me that this was what Cousin Cooper meant by hardness of heart. Contempt. Sheer animal disgust for another human being. Another child of God! So I forced myself to imagine putting my arms around him. Smelling his old clothes. Holding his head on my lap. Even giving him mouth-to-mouth resuscitation."

"*Could* you imagine it? Did you?"

"I did," Sally B. said triumphantly. "I clenched my fists and broke out in a sweat—I swear I had pools of water in my hands—but I did. And afterward a curious thing happened. I looked at him —and he was beautiful. Michelangelo might have painted him."

"You probably had what they call a religious experience," said Vesta.

For a time, as if in retreat from profundities, they chatted of trivial matters. Sally B. poured more tea, which was tepid this time and so strong it puckered their mouths, and, as they drank it—admiring once again the heirloom cups —they gossiped and quipped. At length they returned, without diffidence, to the subject of race.

"I expect you'll give me the usual song and dance," said Vesta, "about how you've nevèr cared for blacks as blacks but just loved them to death as individuals!"

"Not at all," Sally B. said. "Of me, the reverse is true." All her life, she maintained, she had felt deep sympathy for black people in general. Slavery had been a hideous evil. What the race had endured in so-called freedom outraged her sense of justice. The only blacks she'd disliked had been a particular few among whom she'd grown up in Frye's Ferry. "Caesar and his wife aren't bad," she said, "just shiftless. But that Nobie—the one who pieced my quilt—was a stinking tyrant. She'd worked for my grandmother, which gave her a sort of sainthood in the family, and till the day she died, she ruled the roost. She blighted my childhood, interfering with me and bossing me around. And then she had her friends—hèr lodge sisters—who used to come to see her on wet days when I had to play on the back porch. They were skinny old crones with sneery, jaundiced eyes, like starlings. (You can see why I detest those birds.) They'd huddle in a corner of the porch and persecute me."

"How?" asked Vesta, fascinated.

"They talked about me," said Sally B. " 'She ain't pretty, is she?' 'She don't speak up nice 'n' say howdy. Cat got her tongue.' 'Her draw's droops.' 'She don't eat her grits good.' 'She spoiled rotten.' And when I tried not to listen, to lose myself in a dreamworld, they'd cackle out, 'How come you lookin' so popeyed, chile?' " She appealed to Vesta. "Do you think I'm popeyed?"

"Your eyes get round when you're preoccupied, but they don't protrude," said Vesta. "Have you ever tried eye shadow to bring them out at the corners?"

"No, but I will," Sally B. said. "And if I sassed them back, then Nobie reported on me and I had to apologize. The worst crime in Frye's Ferry was to hurt a servant's feelings."

"I'd have killed her," said Vesta.

"Once I bit her," said Sally B.

"Bit her?" Vesta said incredulously.

"It was all I could do. She had me cornered," said Sally B. "One rainy night, the winter I was ten, my mother sent me to get some wood from

112

the kitchen woodbox for the library fire. (We had a gas stove, but Nobie didn't trust it and still cooked on an old wood range.) Nobie was in the kitchen. She didn't say pea-turkey to me till I had my load. Then she grabbed me and said I had to put the wood back in the box—any I wanted I could fetch from the woodhouse, out in the cold rain. I couldn't push her away because my arms were full, so I jolly well bit her on the shoulder till she let me go. Of course, she reported on me."

"Were you punished?"

"I'm still being punished, though not how you think," said Sally B., glowering. "I'd never been a biting child, so my parents were stunned. When they asked me if it could be true, I said —meaning, of course, that I hadn't bitten the blood from Nobie—'Well, she had on her thick union suit.' I knew right then, from the light in my father's eyes, that I'd live to rue those words. Nothing's ever forgotten in our family. Even now, when I disagree with Daddy—about a poem, you know, or a new LP—he'll say, 'But your taste is unique, my dear. *You* like' "—and Sally B. half faltered for a scarcely perceptible fraction of a second—" 'to chew on servants through their undershirts!' "

As she recalled with nostalgia her father's chafing, Sally B. thought how marvelous it was that she could repeat it to Vesta. A feeling of liberation, of having climbed through the dusty trapdoor in the attic into the fresh, broad light of sky, seemed to expand her rib cage. Tomorrow, when she wrote her Sunday letter home, she would describe the sensation. "As with the sexes," she planned to write, "the difference between the races is vastly exaggerated."

But Vesta, whose ear for timing was acute, had caught the hesitation. She was already weary of Mr. Boatwright and his precious sense of humor, and now Sally B.'s obvious editing of his language stung her to the quick. It was a mortifying act of *noblesse oblige*, she felt, that lumped her, Vesta Bethea, with all the touchy menials of Frye's Ferry. "Only he didn't say 'servants,' did he?" she inquired. "Why didn't you use *his* word?" Vesta's tone was dry, needling. Unwillingly, Sally B. was reminded of the carping lodge sisters on the back porch.

"Because it's a coarse word," Sally B. said honestly, "and one I've been taught is not for ladies."

114

"What would the ladies of the Cape Fear region think," asked Vesta, smiling unpleasantly, "if they knew you were drinking tea with me?"

"The ladies of the Cape Fear region couldn't care less what happens in any other part of the world," Sally B. said, with a try for lightness. "Up here, so far from blue water, nothing's too strange to be true."

"Have you ever before? Eaten with one of us, I mean."

"With you," said Sally B. "Three times a day in the dining hall."

"But this is different, isn't it?" said Vesta, driven, by an impulse she did not analyze, to prick Sally B.'s composure. "As an equal. By invitation. A nigger girl using your great-great-granny's white and gold French china!"

"Don't be sickening," said Sally B. She glanced at Vesta's cup. There was a moist smudge of lipstick on it. She glanced away.

Vesta rose. "Well—this was fun," she said. "Before I go, I'll help you wash up."

"No, thanks," said Sally B. "I'll attend to that later." She stooped, took the cups and saucers from the floor, and stepped with them to the trunk beneath the window.

115

"So long, then," said Vesta.

"So long," said Sally B., close to tears.

Now that she knew her thrust had gone home, Vesta was sorry she had pressed it. She lingered, hoping to find some way to make amends. But as she lingered, she saw Sally B. do an odd thing.

First, Sally B. put the dishes on the tray. She did that with care, since they were fragile, but with no more care than was natural. Next, after a long moment of remaining motionless, silhouetted against the window, she retrieved the cups. Grasping them by their delicate handles, she lifted them into midair. Slowly—almost, Vesta felt, as though her hands moved of their own volition—she set them down again, one at either end of the tea tray.

When at last she turned back toward the room, she was still holding her hands wide apart.

"I thought you'd left," she said to Vesta.

"I'm leaving now," Vesta said and was gone.

"No!" Sally B. cried in a choked voice. She ran to the door calling, "Vesta!"

But Vesta had vanished. Amidst the evening noises of the dorm—radios, running water, clamorous voices—even the sound of her feet on the stair was lost.

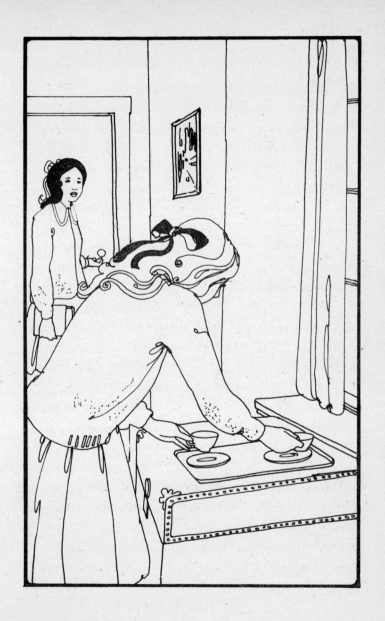

A large, steamy girl in a terry cloth kimono flapped up the hall from the bathroom. "I want you to know I sincerely revere you, Sally B.," she said. "You—a Boatwright from Frye's Ferry —having Vesta Bethea to your room. As an equal. It shows what quality can do."

"Oh, shut up," said Sally B.

Vesta went out of the building, speaking politely to an acquaintance who was coming in, and started across the quadrangle. The air was chilly, now that the sun had set, but less chilly than her heart, and she did not hurry. She walked with studied grace, holding her head high and steady. For a flickering instant, she wondered if her eyes had deceived her, or, if not, and she knew they hadn't, had she drawn a wrong inference from the shadow play at the window? No. The movement of those hands had been impossible to misinterpret. "Animal disgust," Sally B. had said of her aversion to the old scholar.

Vesta shivered. As fragments of the afternoon's talk—"*Our* old Caesar" and "*We* are the people who set the standards"—recurred to her, altered in import, the whole pattern of her life seemed to shift and change. The Victorian house in Queen City—that house with wall-to-wall carpeting and a cut-glass fanlight but no neighbors; the ladies who came there bringing their yard goods—chirping with an effort toward "equality" of manners and confiding in Mrs. Bethea (*Addie* Bethea, they called her) their most intimate problems; the "honor" of being selected for Kenan; the correct, ample wardrobe, packed between sheets of tissue paper in the set of matched luggage (a gift of the Alumni Club) stamped with her initials in gold. Everything that had made her feel proud and secure she now saw as signifying nothing.

But I was never really fooled, she thought. *I always knew security was an illusion. Why did I forget today?*

With shame, Vesta remembered how recklessly she had forgotten. She had exposed her mother to ridicule. For the first time in her life, she had told about the white boys pretending her brother was a dog. And for what purpose? To make friends with a washed-out girl who had no money and no style, whose family had no ambition, a complacent ninny of a girl—a girl who didn't know the meaning of loyalty and was, doubtless, at this minute, regaling her

119

dormitory with a tale of Vesta's cannibal ancestry.

Why did I think I could trust her? Vesta wondered as she reached the crossing of paths where, less than two hours before, she and Sally B. had decided not to part. *Why?*

Because I was lonely, she answered herself. *Because I was too darned lonely to have good sense.*

But what was wrong with loneliness? It was the only real security. It was the garment of kings and poets. Vesta was wrapping herself in loneliness, as in a shawl, when she heard her name called in a plaintive low-country voice.

"Ves-tah! Wait on me, Ves-tah!" called Sally B.

She is coming to apologize, Vesta thought. *The gentry of Frye's Ferry don't wound the feelings of servants.* As she wheeled around, she was trembling but not with cold. Heat flooded into her veins. Her scalp tingled. Automatically she raised a hand to smooth down her hair.

Sally B. was running toward her. Even in the gathering dusk, Vesta could see that her face was deathly pale. Chalky, like a daytime moon.

"I came to say—" Sally B. began when she reached Vesta, who waited with her head flung back and her countenance impassive. But she stopped. For what could she say? That she was sorry she had set the cups apart so as to remember to wash them separately? That she had meant nothing by it? Nothing except that—well, in Frye's Ferry, you know, it was a quaint old custom, a tradition. People down there weren't bigots. They respected blacks. It was simply that they never used the same dishes.

The two girls stood there, eyes fixed on eyes, immobilized by the intensity of their gaze. And as they did, each recognized in the other—Vesta through her blaze of anger and Sally B. through her wretchedness—something of her own secret self. It was the feeling of being a stranger in the world, of staying always poised for retreat, like a doe on the edge of a meadow.

"Yes?" Vesta said, more gently than she'd intended to.

"I came to say—" Sally B. began again, and miraculously, as if a falling star exploded in her mind, an idea came to her—"to say I think we're really obliged to join the demonstration tomorrow. We can't let Padre down, can we? Or ourselves and our principles."

"It's the last thing I want to do," said Vesta.

121

"But I guess you're right. There's no way out of it."

"The one hitch is that I haven't a decent rag to wear," said Sally B. "Could you lend me that yellow cashmere?"

"No," said Vesta. "This is my best sweater. But I have a burnt-orange tweed suit that might look good on you. Come try it on."

Sally B. drew back. "Right now?" she said.

"Right now," said Vesta. "There's no time like the present." She took Sally B.'s hand, which was damp in the palm, and led her down the flagstone path. "And if you'll pardon the free advice," she added, "you'll do well to wear stronger colors. All that blue on a blond grows monotonous."

"I've always worn blue on account of my eyes," said Sally B.

"Sure you have," said Vesta. "And the effect is sweet, in a trite sort of baby-doll way. But, frankly, it isn't what *I* call art!"

The girls began to laugh. They left the narrow path and raced across the grass, light-limbed as dancers, laughing as if they would never stop. *Ha-ha-ha!* Their voices rang in their ears—something like laughter on a printed page.

They Don't Make Glass Slippers Anymore

Lael J. Littke

MY SISTER DARLENE was in love with the boy
who operated the merry-go-round in Erasmus
Park. He had curly black hair and glowing-dark
gypsy eyes. His name was Vincent. It didn't
matter to her that she knew absolutely nothing
else about him.

The only thing was, Vincent didn't pay her a
bit of attention. I guess he was used to the
worship of the girls who brought their brothers,
sisters, cousins, neighbors, or any other available
children to the park so they—the girls—could sit
on the nearby benches and watch him swing
onto the whirling carrousel, collect the tickets
from sticky little hands, and leap gracefully

123

back to his chair, in the center by the controls, which he operated with efficiency and magnificent boredom.

Darlene thought he was divine. She said he looked like a movie star and that the tinny waltzes that came from the innards of the merry-go-round provided a musical background for romance, just like in the movies. She took my brother Arvie and me to the park so often that Arvie became jaded and begged to be allowed to stay home and play with his Tinker Toys.

Consistently, Vincent gave no indication that he ever saw her.

"I can't just walk right up and say, 'My name is Darlene, and I'd like to know you better,' " she said to me one day as we were cleaning up the room we shared.

"Why not?" I asked.

Darlene looked down at me with all the superiority a sixteen-year-old girl can feel over an eleven-year-old sister—and that's quite a lot.

"That just isn't the way you do it," she said slowly and patiently. Then she sighed. "When you grow up, you'll know why not."

"Sure would save a lot of time," I said.

"You don't understand." Darlene flicked a

feather duster across the top of her dressing table, just sort of rearranging the dust. "If I could just get him to notice me!"

"You could leave a glass slipper there next time you go, and then he would come looking for you," I offered. I was a Cinderella fan and considered anything less than princes and ball gowns and fairy godmothers unworthy of being called romance.

Darlene looked at me with something between pity and boredom. "They don't make glass slippers anymore," she said. Putting down the duster, she seated herself at the dressing table and peered at herself in the mirror.

"Mirror, mirror, on the wall," I chanted in a high, squeaky voice, "who is fairest of them all?" Then I shifted to a deep voice to say, "Annalee Ames is the fairest of them all."

Darlene turned around to throw a hairbrush at me. "You think you're so funny!" she said. She turned back to the mirror. "I'm not really bad-looking." Picking up a small bottle of perfume, she sloshed some on her neck. "Darn!" she exploded.

For a second I thought she had dropped the bottle down her front.

"Why didn't I think of that before?" she said. She whirled around on the dressing table bench. "I can't leave a glass slipper, but I could leave my little plastic purse with the set-in rhinestones. I could put my identification card and a lacy handkerchief in it—and maybe fifty cents, so it would seem worth returning. He'd find it and bring it here to me, and, naturally, I'd have to invite him in for a piece of cake, since he'd been so kind."

She leaned her elbows on her knees, day-dreaming.

"Well, let's go," I said.

"Go where?"

"To the park. Your purse isn't going to walk there alone." I looked at her with all the superiority a sensible eleven-year-old girl can feel over her boy-struck older sister—and that, too, is quite a lot!

Darlene jumped to her feet. "Get Arvie," she instructed, dashing to her closet to select a dress.

Arvie, however, didn't want to go. "I'm sick of that merry-go-round," he said.

"You know Mama won't let us go to the park without you," I told him. I think Mama just liked to get us all out of her hair at once.

126

Arvie sighed, but he put away his Tinker Toys.

Mama asked us to pick up a couple of chickens for dinner while we were out. "Be sure to get them at Santuzzi's," she said, "and be back here by five o'clock so I can cook them for dinner."

Mama always bought chickens from Mr. Santuzzi's shop, where the plucked birds were suspended by their legs in the front window, with their heads dangling. Mama said they were fresher there.

We stopped for the chickens on the way to the park. Darlene said she didn't want to take time out on the way home, in case Vincent came right away to return her purse.

When we got to the park, Arvie wanted to play in the sandboxes near the swings. They were on the opposite side of the park from the merry-go-round, and Darlene had to bribe him with cotton candy before he would come with us.

With his black pants, Vincent was wearing an orange shirt, with the first three buttons open, which made him look even more gypsyish and romantic than usual. Darlene put Arvie and me on the merry-go-round for a ride, then found

127

a bench where she could get a good view of Vincent and he could get a good view of her— if he happened to look that way. She had changed her blue jeans and shirt for a scoop-neck white blouse and a full, bright skirt, which she had chosen rather than her straight black skirt and sleeveless black blouse. The black out-fit made her look older and more mysterious, but she figured Vincent's Romany blood would react more to the bright skirt.

As far as I could see, Vincent's Romany blood just lay there, calmly, in his veins. If he noticed Darlene at all, it sure didn't show.

When the merry-go-round stopped, Darlene leaped aboard, before we had a chance to get off.

"Stay on," she hissed, flourishing three tickets. "I'm going to ride, too."

She made Arvie take the inside horse, and she took the middle one, with me on the outside. That way it looked as if she were there to take care of us.

The carrousel started, and our steeds began their monotonous gallop. The music thumped, and Vincent swung onto the moving platform. Darlene licked her lips and adjusted her smile.

She was perched sideways, and she spread her full skirt out to cover her knees. After all, she didn't want to give him the wrong idea—not too much, anyway.

As Vincent approached, Darlene shoved the package of chickens at Arvie. Somehow that lumpy butcher-paper package didn't fit into the image she was trying to create.

Vincent didn't even pause as he took our tickets. He walked right on by, and the bright smile slid slowly from Darlene's face as he moved on to the next row of horses. But she hadn't played her full hand yet.

"Arvie!" she shrieked. "Don't do that! Arvie, you'll fall off!"

Arvie looked at her, puzzled. He was just sitting there, astride his horse, clutching the package of chickens and trying to endure the ride.

Darlene reached over and grabbed his arm. "Arvie!" she shrilled again.

Vincent turned around and came back.

"What's the matter?" he said. He glanced briefly at Darlene, then concentrated on Arvie.

"What's the matter, Bud?" he repeated.

Darlene spoke up breathlessly. "I was afraid he was going to fall off."

129

"He was leaning way over," I put in, trying to be helpful.

Arvie looked at us with all the icy disgust an eight-year-old brother can feel for two crazy sisters—and that's *really* a lot!

"My name isn't Bud," he said to Vincent, with great dignity.

"Well, watch it, Mac," said Vincent. He moved on.

"My name's not Mac!" Arvie shouted, hoarse with rage, but Vincent didn't turn around.

Morosely, Darlene watched Vincent jump off the platform and settle himself in his canvas chair in the center of the merry-go-round. She was too occupied with her own thoughts to watch Arvie, who was swinging the package of chickens around his head by the string. As we passed Vincent, Arvie took careful aim and let fly. The paper came off in midflight, and the two limp, indecently bare chickens, their heads flopping and their stiff feet reaching out for nothing, landed squarely in Vincent's lap, just as the clock in the town hall struck five.

Darlene got off her horse and kept walking around, so that she stayed where Vincent couldn't see her during the rest of the ride. She made me go to retrieve the chickens when the merry-go-round stopped, figuring that Vincent hadn't even looked at me and therefore wouldn't connect either the chickens or me with her or Arvie, whom he most certainly had looked at. She dropped her little purse and hurried away.

I waited until Vincent was looking the other way; then I scooped up the chickens from the ground, where he had thrown them, and ran. I stopped only long enough to grab up the paper, which I wrapped loosely around the birds before handing them to Arvie to carry. He carried them gingerly by the legs and lost the paper somewhere along the street.

"If he saw who threw those chickens, he won't ever come," Darlene said, her voice quivery, as if she were going to cry. But she said we would take the bus home, since she wanted to be sure to be there in case he did come.

We nodded to Mr. Harris, the bus driver, as we got on. None of us said anything until we had been riding for about three blocks. Then Arvie said, "I'm sick."

The cotton candy, the merry-go-round, the swaying of the bus, and the sight of the chickens lying there on his lap, their dead eyes half-open and their bodies cold and blue, were too much for Arvie. He tossed the chickens onto the empty seat across the way, groaned weakly, and lay down. Darlene told me to open a window, while she started fanning him with her hands.

In the excitement, we left the chickens on the bus.

"How could you possibly lose two chickens?" demanded Mama when we arrived home, pale and empty-handed.

"My life may be ruined, and I should worry about chickens?" asked Darlene.

"Well, dinner may be ruined, too!" said Mama. "Those chickens were for dinner."

Arvie went a little paler and ran to his room to lie down.

"Who wants to eat?" said Darlene. She was starting up the stairs, when the doorbell rang. Suddenly she was Cinderella, waiting for her prince. Her eyes, which had been filling with tears, sparkled with excitement.

"It's Vincent," she whispered. "He did come, anyway." She sprinted to the door and flung it open. There stood a skinny twelve-year-old with buck teeth. In his outstretched hand, he held Darlene's little purse.

"Vincent said to take this to the goofy dame with the bratty brother and the dead chickens," he said.

Darlene just stood there.

"Thanks," I said, snatching the purse and slamming the door. The doorbell rang again. The kid was still there, his hand still outstretched. "Cost me fifteen cents on the bus," he said.

Darlene opened the purse and handed him the fifty cents she had put in it. I slammed the door again.

"Well, so much for Cinderella," I said.

"I want to die," whispered Darlene. She sank dramatically into a chair near the door.

Mother, who had been watching the whole scene, said, "Well, before you do, will you go get a couple more chickens?" She went into the kitchen.

I was standing by Darlene's side, patting her back and hoping I'd never be sixteen, when the doorbell rang again. When I opened the door, I saw a tall blond boy with the bluest eyes I had ever seen. He held a package wrapped neatly in newspapers.

"Is your sister here?" he asked.

"Darlene," I said.

133

She got to her feet, tragedy still lining her face. She stared glassily at the boy.

"Hi," he said. "I brought your chickens." He handed the package to her. "I was behind you on the bus, but I didn't see the chickens until you got off. The bus driver told me where you live."

Darlene continued to stare at him, now with awakening interest.

"My name is Jeff," the boy said. "My family just moved in down the street." He grinned down at her rather shyly.

That was when Darlene came to completely. A dazzling smile erased the tragedy from her face.

"Why, Jeff," she said, "come on in and have a piece of cake. Since we're neighbors now, we may as well get acquainted."

"I think so, too," Jeff said happily.

As they headed for the kitchen, I went upstairs to tell Arvie he was a regular fairy godmother. After that, I planned to reread my favorite version of Cinderella.

The Year of the Baby

Carol Madden Adorjan

IT'S NOT ENOUGH that she had her hair frosted!"
Lorna exclaimed, crumpling her lunch bag.

"You'll get used to it," Debbie said.

Lorna grimaced. "And her clothes! All *kinds*
of mod things. I'm telling you, she's flipped!"

Debbie laughed.

"Everybody keeps telling her how beautiful
she looks—how radiant. And she loves it!"

The bell sounded through the cafeteria, and
the girls pushed back their chairs.

"Wouldn't you?" Debbie dropped her bag
into the container by the door. "The day somebody tells me I'm beautiful is the day I'll—well,
I don't know what I'll do." She sighed. "But I

135

have a feeling I'll have lots of time to think of something."

They went into the cool green corridor and fell into line.

"But my mother's nearly forty!" Lorna exclaimed. "She's too old for frosted hair and—"

Debbie's smile was wry. "That's not what's really bothering you, is it?" With that, she drifted off toward her locker and disappeared into the crowd.

Annoyance gnawed at Lorna. Debbie had a way of tossing the ball and disappearing before it could be returned.

Of course it bothered her. The hair, the clothes —they were part of the total picture. How would Debbie feel, she wondered, if *her* mother had announced blithely, one night after dinner, that life was never again going to be the same? The scene was painfully vivid, even now.

She knew immediately that something had happened when she burst through the kitchen door, still excited over the reaction her speech had received in English class. Her mother nodded and smiled, but Lorna had a feeling she wasn't really listening. There was something different about her mother—about everything!

136

For one thing, her father was home. He was rarely home before Lorna. And they were having hot dogs and beans—something her father despised—for the second time in a week.

"Beans? Again?" Lorna asked. "How come?"

Her mother stirred the beans slowly over the stove. "I just got home myself. There wasn't time to prepare anything else." Even her voice was different. Excited. Tremulous.

Lorna searched her mother's face for some clue. But she only smiled at her fleetingly and turned to the cabinet. "Put your books away and hang up your coat. I could use your help." She counted out three plates and set them on the table.

Lorna crossed the kitchen and passed through the dining room, where her father sat reading his paper. Behind him, the last light of the afternoon washed her mother's easel and the unfinished painting in an eerie golden glow.

"Not even a hello for your old dad?" her father said.

"Oh, hi, Dad," Lorna answered. "Home early, huh?"

He looked different, too. A strange, mysterious grin turned up the corners of his mouth and

137

seemed to spill into his eyes. Lorna could feel him watching her as she went into the hall.

She closed her bedroom door behind her and stood against it, trying to understand why she felt so deflated. She had practically floated home, buoyant with success. But the minute she had walked in the door, she had felt the air going out of her, until now there was nothing but this sinking sensation in the pit of her stomach—this curious sense of foreboding. She dropped her books on her desk. "Silly," she reprimanded herself. "You come home, and your mother acts a little peculiar, and you get all upset. Silly. Silly. Silly."

Still, she delayed leaving her room until her mother's call seeped through the door.

"Be right there," she answered, trying on a smile.

In the kitchen, she took up the silverware and began to set the table. "I wish you had been there," she said, trying to recapture her previous excitement. "Miss Abernathy is not overly free with the compliments, to say the least; she's never done more than just nod when I gave a speech, but today!"

Her father came to the kitchen door. "How do

138

you like your mother's hair?"

Lorna wheeled around to face her mother. Her hair! Was that it? "Your hair!" she exclaimed, relief flooding her. "Was that all—I mean, I knew there was something different, but— It's all blond!"

Her mother laughed. "Not all of it." She patted her hair self-consciously. "Here and there. They call it frosting. Do you like it?"

"It's beautiful," Lorna assured her. "You look younger!"

Her mother smiled into the pan of hot dogs. "Do you really think so?" She filled the plates and put them on the table.

Marveling at the sparkle in her mother's eyes and the way her pale skin seemed almost translucent, Lorna said, "You look so—different!"

Her father smiled fondly at her mother. "It's not just the hair."

The sense of foreboding fluttered once more inside Lorna, like a flag of warning. "What do you mean?"

"Your mother has something to tell you."

Her mother glanced at her and lowered her eyes. "Oh, John," she demurred, "it'll keep until after supper."

"You said you couldn't wait until Lorna came home so you could tell her."

"I know, but. . . ."

Despite her uneasiness, Lorna laughed. "*Some*body tell me!"

They turned smiling eyes on her; both began to speak at once, laughed, and fell silent. Finally her mother blurted, "We're going to have a baby, Lorna. Isn't that wonderful?"

Lorna froze, with her fork in midair. Fiery flashes of confusion exploded on her cheeks and in her stomach. She tittered uneasily. "A baby? You're kidding!"

"No," her mother said. "In the spring. Such a lovely time. You were born on the first day of spring. Well, night, really. Remember?" She laughed. "No, of course you don't. It was so beautiful. Warm, with a breeze, and the stars scattered overhead like jewels. I'll never forget. . . ."

Her mother went on talking, but Lorna didn't hear. *A baby*, she kept thinking. *A baby!* She could hear him crying and see him wriggling, and she hated him.

"Lorna?" her mother was saying.

Lorna looked up. They were staring at her.

140

Under the puzzlement in their eyes, she shifted uncomfortably.

"Won't it be great?" her father asked.

"Great," Lorna said, trying to suppress a facetious inflection. "Just great."

"You've always wanted a brother or sister." Her mother's voice was flat. "We thought you'd be so pleased."

"Oh, I am. It's great. Really." She pushed herself away from the table. "I have a lot of homework. Would you mind if I didn't help with the dishes tonight?"

"Now, wait a minute, young lady," her father began, but her mother put her hand over his.

"If you have homework," she said, "you'd better do it."

Lorna had gone down the hall to her room not thinking anything. She felt numb. It was a joke. It had to be. In a minute, her mother would come in and tell her it wasn't true.

When she didn't come, Lorna opened her math book and stared down at the meaningless symbols that marched across the page.

A *baby!* Her whole life would be changed. Didn't they know that? Or, more important, didn't they care? She was fourteen. An only child. She had grown accustomed to that, and she liked it.

Oh, there had been times when she'd wished more than anything for a sister or brother, someone near her own age with whom she could share a rainy day, but that was a long time ago. It was too late for that now. Besides, there were compensations. There had never been any need to hide her diary, as Debbie had to do, or to remember not to leave anything valuable down low, where little hands could get at it. Her room —anyplace in the house, really—was safe territory. Her room! What *about* that? Certainly they didn't expect her to share it with a squalling, red-faced— No, that would be too much!

"The whole thing is too much," Lorna told Debbie one day after school as they sidestepped a tangle of baby carriages that lined the shopping center walk. "I mean, everywhere you look —babies!"

They ordered sodas in the malt shop and thumbed through magazines as they waited.

"You'd think change was a disease or something," Debbie said.

"Well, the symptoms aren't very pleasant," Lorna countered. She thought of her mother's

143

sudden preoccupation with things domestic: her insistence that every cabinet and closet be scrubbed clean; the tangled balls of pastel yarn that turned up on tabletops and underfoot; the grainy homemade bread that sat squarely on the dinner table and her mother's hopeful "It's better than the last batch, don't you think?"

"She calls it 'nesting,' " Lorna said. "I call it disaster."

"When does she find time to paint?" Debbie asked.

Lorna hedged. Her mother hadn't picked up a brush in weeks, and that's what disturbed her most. The abandoned picture her mother called *Modern Madonna*, flat and colorless these days in the gray winter light that filtered through the dining room window, was the most constant reminder of impending change.

Every day when Lorna arrived home, she hoped to see her mother standing at the easel, the familiar blue paint-spattered shirt hanging loosely about her slim shoulders. She had never taken her mother's painting seriously. Even her mother admitted that she was certainly no artist. But somehow Lorna felt that if she had added even a stroke to the barely discernible baby in

144

the painting, everything would be all right again.

But her mother was never there. Instead, she was at the hairdresser's or bent awkwardly over the oven or lying down in the darkened living room.

Through it all, her mother was irritatingly gay. She hummed and chattered and made jokes about her inability to knit an entire row without a mistake.

Even her father had changed. There was a new buoyancy to his walk. Often he tousled her hair and called her "Princess," something he hadn't done since Lorna was very little.

It was stifling! And as the weeks passed and her mother, despite her frosted hair, began looking like a photograph from the *National Geographic*, with her spindly arms and legs and her distended middle, Lorna spent more and more time away from home.

"I wish I could just move out," Lorna sighed as she fell back across Debbie's bed.

Debbie pulled a sweater over her head. "Where would you go?"

"Anywhere. It wouldn't matter. I don't suppose they'd even miss me."

"Come off it, will you?"

Debbie's five-year-old brother flung himself into the room and careened into her.

"Don't you ever knock?" Debbie demanded as she regained her balance.

"They're after me!" he exclaimed.

Debbie took hold of his shoulders and steered him toward the door. "Well, they won't find you here!" She pushed him into the hall and slammed the door.

"How do you stand it?" Lorna asked.

"You get used to it. Except the noise." She slipped into her skating socks. "On second thought, I guess you get used to that, too. The few times I've come into the house when no one's been here—well, it's awful. So quiet. I can never stay in it unless I turn on the radio or something."

Lorna slung her skates over her shoulder and followed Debbie to the door. "Somewhere quiet. That's where I'd move!"

At the skating pond, Lorna hooked her fingers into her skate laces and tugged to tighten them. "It wouldn't be so bad, I suppose, if my mother didn't act as if she were the only one in the world who'd ever had a baby."

146

In the center of the warming house, Debbie held her hands over the glowing coals of the potbellied stove. "And if you'd quit acting as if you were the only one whose world was going to change. . . ."

Confusion chilling her, Lorna watched her friend toe across the planked floor and out the door.

"What was that supposed to mean?" she challenged, skating up beside Debbie.

Grinning, Debbie executed a smooth turn and glided off. "If people would open their eyes sometimes, instead of their mouths. . . ."

Lorna decided against pursuing the meaning of that remark. She skated off, giving herself gladly to the stinging breeze she created as she raced across the pond.

Later, when she turned into her walk, the streetlights flickered on and a light snow began to collect around their bases. The house was dark and unnaturally quiet for this time of day, and Lorna conceded that Debbie was right about one thing: Silence had a deafening sound of its own.

In the middle of the dining room, she halted. Despite the darkness, she sensed a change in

147

the room. She turned slowly. The easel, with its unfinished picture, was gone. A queer sense of panic traveled her spine, like a current through a wire.

"Mother?" she called. In the kitchen, she flipped on the light. A lid danced on a steaming pot, and the refrigerator buzzed. "Mother!"

She heard a rustle of movement overhead and hurried into the hall. The attic door was open. Lorna started up the narrow staircase, blinking against the pungent odor of camphor and musty newspaper.

Her mother looked down from the top of the stairs. "I didn't realize it was so late," she said. "I was going to have some nice hot chocolate waiting for you." Her mouth smiled, but there were tears in her voice. "How was skating?"

In the small, dimly lit room, the clutter cast weird shadows against the slanted ceiling. "Are you all right?" Lorna asked.

Her mother turned. "All right? Of course. Why wouldn't I be all right?"

As her eyes grew accustomed to the dimness, Lorna saw the empty easel leaning against a white crib. In a corner, canvases leaned against one another, their faces to the wall.

148

"I've been getting some things ready," her mother explained, with a wave of her hand.

Lorna ran her hand along the crib rail. It was dusty.

"I'm afraid I didn't get very far," her mother said. "There are so many things to do." She lowered herself into a cane-backed rocker. "So many things."

Lorna sat on the corner of a trunk. Though her mother's face was shadowed, Lorna could see the weariness there—and something else. Uncertainty? Had it been there all these months, thinly veiled under the quick smile?

She dismissed the faint glimmer of guilt that swung toward her, poking light into the dark corners of her mind, and focused on the old blue shirt her mother wore.

"Have you been painting?"

Her mother's laugh was hollow. "I haven't picked up a brush since— I have a feeling I may never paint again."

"But why? You love to paint!"

Her mother stood beside the crib. "Would you believe you slept in this? It didn't take long, though, before you grew too big for it. Things change."

In this half-light, her mother looked rather like an unfinished painting herself—as though something were missing—as though the artist had lost touch with the original idea and given up. "What's wrong, Mom?"

Her mother shook her head. "Nothing, really. I got to thinking today how different things will be after the baby's here. It's been such a long time...."

Lorna was incredulous. "You mean . . . you don't *want* the baby?" She bit back the word *either*.

Her mother sat beside her. "Oh, I want the baby," she said, taking Lorna's hand into her own. "Very much! But—sometimes things seem to pile up so that, instead of a hill, there's a mountain to climb. And, truthfully, I don't know if I have the wind for it."

Debbie's words, *And if you'd quit acting as if you were the only one whose world was going to change*, dashed across her mind, spilling new meanings.

It wasn't the baby at all. It never had been. It was the panic she felt in the face of change. Apparently *everybody* felt that sooner or later. Sometimes you had to remind yourself that

150

change wasn't a tragedy but a condition of life. Probably the one thing that never changed was that everything kept changing. Feeling curiously relieved, Lorna turned to her mother. "Where will we put him?"

"Your father's always wanted to add dormers up here to make it a real room. In the meantime—"

"In the meantime, how about my room?"

Her mother patted Lorna's hand and averted her eyes. "Oh, dear!" she said suddenly. "The soup!" She used the corner of the crib to pull herself up and waddled toward the stairs. "Coming?"

"Where's the Madonna?" Lorna asked.

"Over there, with the others."

Lorna checked the nearest canvas and lifted it to the easel so that it faced the crib.

"Someday I'll have to finish it," her mother said softly.

"You will." Lorna stood back and cocked her head in silent appraisal. "All it needs is the baby."

The Summer of Charley Crip

Suzanne Roberts

SHE HEARD IT very early in the morning, the unmistakable cheep-cheep of a baby bird crying to be fed. At the sound, just one thought crowded her mind: *Kevin!*

It wasn't, of course, that she forgot that Kevin was dead. It had been six months now, and no longer did she wake up in the morning thinking that he was there, in his own room down the hall . . . that she would be fighting with him over who got the bathroom first . . . that he would be teasing her about some boy she had a crush on. "What are big brothers for," her mother used to say, "if not to tease little sisters? You mustn't take it seriously, Karry, dear. . . ."

She didn't forget anymore that she would never see him again. His face would dim in her memory, and one day, perhaps when she was old, she might not even be able to recall the sound of his laugh or his voice in anger or feel again the sweet pride she used to feel because he was so smart and so popular at school and he was her brother—hers.

Now, turning her face on the pillow, she saw that it was still very early; the sun was just coloring the lake a lovely shade of pink. Early mornings at the lake used to be very special times. When they were smaller—Kevin too young to shave and Karry so little that she still lugged that old rag doll around—they would get up before anybody else and go down to the beach to watch goldeneyes and old-squaws flying in across the water. Even then, Kevin knew a lot about birds. Standing importantly on the freshly painted pier, his eyes very blue and serious as he talked to her, he would point out the differences between the ducks.

The sound of the frantic, hungry baby bird continued. Karry finally got up, reaching for her jeans and sneakers and old terry cloth shirt. Dressed, she walked through the chilly, sleeping cottage to the front porch.

The view hadn't changed—not in all the years she remembered. The rushes were still there, and the cottages far across the lake, and the shadowed trees out on the island, where teenagers, Kevin included, used to go for bonfires and parties last summer. That had been the summer he went into the Marines. He had promised her that this summer, when he came home on leave, he would save one night just for her, and they would sit someplace quiet and talk, and he would tell her just what it felt like to be in a war—to be fighting a real war.

She closed her eyes for a second; then, when she opened them, she deliberately looked away from the lake and the wooded island. There were trees, big ones, in front of nearly every cottage on the lakeshore. The baby bird might have fallen from its nest.

The cheeping, by the time she got there, was very loud, almost a screech. She stood on tiptoe, trying to see, and it was exactly at that moment that she heard the sound of the truck. She turned, just in time to see a dark green pickup with something painted on its side take off down the road.

Karry began to make a loud crooning noise, the kind that Kevin and she used to make when they'd drag a ladder from tree to tree, looking for eggs—not to steal or even touch but just to gaze at. That had been years ago, before he grew up and got busy with girls and decided to go into the Marines, but Karry could still make the sound, deep in her throat.

She was standing under the old elm, looking up and crooning, when the boy came around the side of the house. Karry wouldn't have noticed him, because he was barefoot and the grass was high and soft, but he called out to her.

"Hey," he said, "is there a cat caught up there or something?"

She turned to look at him. He was tall and skinny, and he had dark hair and a thin, serious face. "Not a cat," she said, her voice edged with unfriendliness. "It's a bird."

She turned her back to him; she didn't want any new friends. Back home, she had deliberately dropped out of all her old school activities. She wasn't sure why. It had nothing to do with the kind of formal mourning her grandmother had done for Kevin. It was more like a rage inside her, buried, hidden deep, so that

155

she only wanted to be left alone. It was because of this—this secret, terrible anger in her—that her parents had decided it might be best, after all, to come to the lake cottage for the summer, just as they had done for so many years. Her father could drive back and forth to work during the week. Besides, her mother had said softly, Kevin would have wanted them to go on living and be happy, wouldn't he?

"A bird," the boy behind her said, his voice both arrogant and shy. "Sure is noisy for a bird." He moved closer to her. She glanced at him, wishing he would go away, and she saw that his faded blue shirt had the word *Pendalton* printed on the back of it. He stood away from her, peering up at the tree, his back half-turned. Suddenly he swung around, his eyes narrowed, as if to catch her at something. They stared at each other, two wary strangers, and finally he shoved his hands into his jeans pockets.

"If you're scared of me," he said quietly, "don't be. I work here for Mrs. Mason. I'm painting her boathouse and doing yardwork and stuff." There was something in his eyes that begged her for something. She struggled for a second, trying to decide what it was, and then, when

156

he turned quickly at the sound of a screen door
opening and slamming shut, she knew. Of course
—Pendalton. She watched him walk quickly
away from her, his long, spidery legs funny-
looking in the faded old work pants. Pendalton—
that was the boys' correctional home at Nautum,
on the other side of the lake.

She squinted a little, for the sun was coming
up full and hot now, and went back to the cottage to get a ladder, so she could see what was
happening with that noisy little bird.

"I just don't like it, Jack," her mother said
to her father. The three of them were sitting in
the cottage kitchen. None of them had grown
used to three places instead of four being set.
Her mother had said, when Kev first went into
the Marines, that she would never get used to
three places, but it had been different then. He
had only gone away to Texas to boot camp.

"Margaret," her father said patiently, in that
special, soft, very kind voice he had used to her
ever since Kev died, "it's perfectly all right,
honey. Those boys, the ones who work outside
that way, are on that new honor system. Besides,
I don't think the kids they put in that place have

157

done anything really terrible."

"It just makes me sick," her mother said, in a small, shaking voice, "when I think of our boy and what happened and how good he was, and then here's a boy they had to put in one of those correctional places because he—"

"Margaret," her father said, "we don't *know* what that boy did!" He changed the subject abruptly, turning to Karry and pretending interest in the bird she had taken from the nest. "What're you planning to do with that bird, honey? He sure makes a lot of noise!"

Her father knew nothing about birds or any of the other things that used to be so important to Kevin, but, because they were important to Kev, they had become important to Karry, too. When she had taken that naked, beady-eyed cowbird from the warbler's nest, she had felt quite sure Kev would have wanted her to do just that. The big egg had been covered up by the mother warbler, and it was a miracle that it had hatched at all. That meant that the mother warbler didn't want to feed it, and, after all, there was no reason that she should, since this big ugly thing wasn't her baby. Its own mother, sneaky thing that she was, had pulled the age-

158

old trick of cowbirds. She had deposited her egg in another bird's nest, hoping the other mother wouldn't know the difference. But this one had, so if Karry hadn't come along, the baby cowbird would probably have starved.

He sounded as if he were starving all the time. Karry put him in an upside-down plastic clothes basket, the kind with holes in it, so that he could see out, and she lined the floor of his cage with soft grass and dried rush. She wasn't at all sure what he needed or what to feed him, except worms, but the worms didn't surface unless it rained, and the weather had been clear and dry lately. It was nearly afternoon before she remembered what she must do first.

There had been a summer, five years ago, at least, when she and Kev had found a goldeneye on the beach. She must have been around eleven then, too big to drag the rag doll about but still young enough to stand in awe of Kev because he was a teen-ager.

That was the day she learned to tell the difference between the goldeneyes and the old-squaws. When they were in the air, you couldn't really tell which was which, but this particular morning, when Kevin had suddenly broken into a run, she had hurried after him, toward the old pier near Devon's boathouse. Ducking under the pier, she found out that goldeneyes really do have golden eyes.

The duck had been caught under the pier. Kev told her it was hurt, and that was all he told her. She could hear the poor thing squawking, whether in pain or fear, she didn't know. Her brother held it gently in both of his strong hands and talked to it in a calm, low voice. She had edged closer, a little afraid of the creature. They were bigger than she had thought, these ducks, but very beautiful, with pure white throats and breasts and sleek, dark brown heads. This one's eyes, as they turned toward her in sheer panic, were the color of amber wine.

"Go on back," Kevin had told her firmly. He had always bossed her, and she had nearly always obeyed him, but this time she stood there, in frozen, fascinated horror, for the bird had only one leg, and where the other had been, there was only a tiny, bloody, footless stem.

"Go on back, Karry," her brother had said again, in a sterner tone. "You don't want to look at him. He's hurt bad."

"He's only got one leg left," she had said

stupidly. Then, unaccountably, she had burst into tears.

But she hadn't gone back to the cottage. Instead, she had sat on the sun-warmed sand and watched her brother carefully examine the wounded bird, turning him this way and that, holding shut the squawking bill, and gently stroking the lovely, sleek head.

"Well," he had said finally, "he can't fly like this. Can't get his landing gear up—not with this darned thing dangling that way." He had looked at his sister, his blue eyes steady. "You go on back," he had said quietly and kindly. "You go on back now, Karry."

Something, some kind of dread, had arisen in her, making her heart pound. Strange—that same feeling had come back to her that winter night she had been awakened by Sandi's mother. She had gone to a fudge party at her best friend's house, and sometime in the middle of the night, Sandi's mother had come into the bedroom and called Karry's name. "You must go home, honey. Something has happened, and they want you home right away. We'll drive you."

The something that had happened was the

news of Kev. And on the way home, sitting bundled in Sandi's mom's car, the windshield wipers had sung the song, making it certain for her, turning the feeling of fear and dread into absolute certainty. *Kevin is dead; Kevin is dead; Kevin is dead. . . .*

That morning, when Kevin had cut off the pitiful, dangling piece of leg, carefully binding it tightly and talking all the while to the fluttering, squawking bird, she had grown up. She had not gone back to the cottage to hide her eyes; she had stayed by her brother's side, not even crying, not getting sick, saying some little secret prayers for the poor thing. Then, when it was over, she had watched her wonderful brother fill an eyedropper with sweet, cool well water and put it into the bird's mouth again and again.

Yes! she thought now. *Everything needs water, even before food!* So water from an eyedropper was the first thing the baby cowbird got. He got milk-soaked bread, too, but still he cried most of the day.

In the evening, when her parents had gone out in the old rowboat to fish, Karry went back down toward the warbler's nest, where she had

162

found the unwanted cowbird. Mrs. Warbler had hatched her own brood and was very busy attending them. She was giving them worms, Karry noticed, so surely there must be night crawlers around someplace.

"Hullo," the boy said from behind her. He was barefoot this time, too, and his face was sunburned. He had developed some freckles, or else she hadn't noticed them before. He grinned at her, his eyes showing that same mixture of defiance and eagerness that she had puzzled over before. "Did you lose something?"

"No," she said coolly. "I'm looking for worms." When he didn't go away, she turned and looked up into his face. She really didn't want to be friendly with him, but there he was, not budging, standing there as if he were determined to find out what she was up to. "I have a bird," she said, as patiently as she could. "I have to feed him, and I can't find any worms."

"I'll find them," he said, and immediately he was on his hands and knees, digging with his fingers. He had some freckles on his hands, too, she noticed, and he needed a haircut. Something in her began to feel a kind of ease, a feeling she had no idea how to explain. "You have

163

to come very early in the morning," he said, his head bent over his digging, "like the early bird." He flashed her a quick look, to see if she thought his little joke was funny. Seeing her unsmiling eyes, he went quickly back to his digging.

He did find some worms, though. He also found a can in the shed belonging to the lady he worked for. Together he and Karry patted dirt into the can, and together they leaned over the lake's edge and scooped up small amounts of water by hand, to moisten the dirt in the can.

They were still doing that, near the old pier, when the truck came. It honked rudely, shattering the almost pleasant silence that had been theirs, hers and the boy's—Lang's.

"I have to go," he said, his voice suddenly ashamed. "They bring us and pick us up. Maybe I'll see you tomorrow."

"Maybe," she said, and she remembered what her mother had said—about how Kevin had died fighting a war, while this boy had to be put away because he'd done something awful. "Maybe not," she added. She stood up, turning her back to him, still holding the can of dark, wet earth filled with worms.

Sometime in the night, she had decided not

164

to speak to Lang again. But the next morning, when she saw him working on the boat he was supposed to clean up and paint, she found herself walking down that way. She had the cowbird baby in her hand, her fingers gently pressed against its wings so it wouldn't flutter out and fall.

"I brought the bird," she said.

His blue eyes lit up with pleasure, and he very carefully put down the can of paint and the brush. Then, after peering at the naked, ugly, beady-eyed little thing from every possible angle and touching it with his sunburned, freckled hand, he finally straightened up and said gravely, "That's a real fine bird you've got there. Want to feed him some more worms? I can get all you want."

So, together, they sat on the old pier in the morning sunlight, putting one wiggly worm after another into the screeching, greedy little mouth until finally—finally—the sharp black eyes closed, and the baby bird slept, warm and secure in Karry's moist, gentle hand.

Just before lunchtime, she walked over to the boat, where he had gone back to work, and settled herself on the pier. He turned to glance

165

at her, his eyes pleased, and it was then that she asked the question.

"Lang? What did you do? What did you do that made them put you in that place?"

His eyes changed, deepening with discomfort and shame.

"I stole a car," he said abruptly. "Took it all the way to Florida. I was going to have me a high old time, I guess, only they caught me." He looked at her steadily, waiting, Karry knew, to see if she would get up, turn her back, and walk away forever. "Somehow," he said slowly, "I don't think of myself as a thief anymore. I guess anybody can make a mistake—anybody."

Surprised, she heard herself say, "Yes." She was angry with herself for saying it, because she did not, simply did not, want to be friends with him. What was it she wanted from him, then? She didn't know, unless maybe enough worms for the baby bird. She didn't much like looking for worms—digging in the earth, getting it under her nails, picking up the worms, all slimy and squirmy, knowing every one would soon be eaten by the greedy little bird.

Lang would come in the truck in the mornings and work until noon; then he would eat his lunch

from a brown paper sack, sitting in the shade near the old pier, his funny-looking skinny legs stretched out in front of him. It was during one noontime that he built the cage for the baby bird, using old strips of wood that had dried out in the hot June sun. Together he and Karry admired it, and together they exclaimed over the fact that the baby bird was getting feathers, soft and downy. He had some even on his naked little head, and together they laughed when the head popped up and the black eyes stared brightly at them, with the new feathers on the head comically sticking right straight up.

"He ought to have a name," Lang told her one afternoon. They'd been swimming at the cove; Lang had gotten permission from the lady he worked for at the cottage. "Everything ought to have a name if it can," he said. "It makes it more . . . dignified."

So they named the cowbird Baby. It was a silly name, but it suited him very well. He had begun to walk around after Karry, squawking, obviously thinking that she was his mother. Finally Karry and Lang began to worry about him, because he hadn't flown yet.

On a hot day at the beginning of July, they

gave Baby a flying lesson. He could fly, all right. The only trouble was that he'd just circle around and come straight back to Karry.

"I guess he loves you," Lang said, and he quickly turned away from her and began digging for the endless supply of worms that Baby needed.

On the Fourth, the holiday, the truck didn't bring Lang, and Karry and her parents and some neighbors sat in the yard facing the blue lake, watching the neighbor children burning sparklers. Karry thought of Kevin, suddenly realizing that she had not thought of him with the same sadness and intensity that she used to. This made her feel guilty, somehow. He mustn't ever be pushed out of her mind or heart, because then, she knew, he would really be gone. He would really be lost, if nobody remembered him.

It rained a lot that month, and for nearly a week, the green Pendalton truck did not bring Lang. Karry was very restless, but when the weather got nice again, the truck came. She said little to Lang; still, they were togther a lot, sitting on the pier, swimming, looking for worms, discussing the fate of Baby.

"You ought to let him go," Lang said one day.

169

It was August, and already the nights were cool, and flocks of old-squaws, their greenish hooded heads gleaming in the sunlight, could be seen migrating. There were some goldeneyes with them, all of them in formation, flying close to avoid the duck hawks.

Karry held Baby close to her. He was comfortably full of worms, and he sat on her lap, feathered and fat and content.

"No," she said, and her tone was sharp. "I'm going to keep him. When we go back to the city, I'm going to take him with me. My parents said I could."

Lang shook his head. "It's not right," he said, not looking at her but instead staring across the lake. "To lock him up, not to let him be free— it's bad. He hasn't done anything. He ought to be free, the way he wants to be."

They had never argued, but now her voice grew loud with anger.

"You don't know anything at all! You don't know about the hawks and the hunters and all the rest of the things that could kill him! He'd never make it," she said, and her finger felt for the tiny beating heart of the bird on her lap. "I'm not going to let him die," she said. "I'm not

170

going to let them kill him!''

It was an argument, an argument that grew into a breach between them that could not be healed. No more did she go to the cottage where he worked. No more did she manufacture excuses to spend time with him. If she happened to see him on the beach, she quickly looked the other way.

The days were getting cooler, and many of the summer people had already packed up and gone back to the city. Lang came to say good-bye to her one cool August morning as Karry sat on the pier. He suddenly came up behind her, and she sensed his presence and turned around to look into his lonely, angry blue eyes.

"I'm leaving," he said. "They're letting me go home, back to my folks. I don't suppose you would want me to call you up or anything."

She held Baby closer. It did little good to get attached to living, breathing things—very little good. In fact, it made no sense at all, because you always lost them. They died or they went away. She held the bird closer to her, stroking its head. "Good-bye," she said, and that was all.

It was then that the duck flock circled and swooped and came down to feed. Karry and

171

Lang watched them in strained silence as the green truck came down the road very fast, to pick up Lang. Karry felt tears in her eyes, but she didn't look around.

Then she saw him! He was big and fine-looking, with his sleek brown head and pure white breast. He seemed to be the leader of the others, eating first, hopping around on his one leg, making the other males stand to one side for him.

Karry stood up. It had to be! And she remembered the name her brother had given him, because he, too, like Lang, thought that living things should be graced with the dignity of a name. *Charley—Charley Crip.*

She stood watching as the flock took off, Charley Crip first, the leader, soaring ahead of them all, straight for the sun, his whole body gleaming. They did not always die, then. You loved them and did what you could, and God had to do the rest.

She stood holding Baby, and then, very quickly, she opened her two hands and let him go. He seemed to hesitate for a second, but then he flew away, alone, heading by instinct to where there would be other cowbirds. He would mate, and his mate would lay her egg in another bird's nest, because that was their way, and maybe somebody would find it and cherish it, just as Karry had found and cherished Baby.

She let her hands drop to her sides, and then she took a small breath, watching the beautiful bird fly free at last. Now Karry knew what it was that she had received from her dead brother. He had taught her how to be a good friend and how to share and how to be honest. And from these precious gifts, she could go beyond, into the world of grown-up love, into the world of being a young woman with compassion, instead of a selfish child who hugged grief to herself, like an old rag doll.

She turned around to smile into Lang's eyes. Now she was strangely free—free of her anger and free of her sadness.

Debbie Faces Herself

Pauline Smith

I AM A TYPICAL TEEN-AGER. I mean I *was* a typical teen-ager—the kind whose parents scream, "For heaven's sake, Debbie, turn off that blaring nonmusic and clean up your room," or, "You are not stepping a foot from this house, young lady, until you've done those dishes your mother asked you to do."

It was very discouraging being a typical teen-ager. If you want the actual truth, it was *dismal*, with all those commands and complaints! Not that my brother, who is a year younger and deserves it, didn't get the same treatment. He did: "Jerry! You stop dribbling that basketball and get to the lawn." Also, "March straight back

174

into the house, young man, and wax that kitchen floor for your mother."

Then they ended up telling Jerry what a typical teen-ager he was, which was okay by him, but when they told *me* that, I brooded, because if this was it, I didn't want to be typical.

Suddenly, though, Mom became a typical mother, which my mother has never been. What I mean is, she was *gone*. Every kid I know has a mother who is not waiting at home after school but, instead, is off playing bridge or shopping or at the Women's Club or somewhere.

I always thought that would be kind of nice, you know? I could turn my record player up loud, loll around in my school clothes, telephone my friends, live it up casually, and not have to snap to it on the homework or pick up every little thing in my room. That's what I thought —it might be fun not having Mom there. But when she started *not* being there, it was kind of worrisome, you know?

"Where do you go, for gosh sakes?" I asked her, after a few times of coming home to an empty house and not having to do anything. "You've always been here before."

She gave me a funny kind of smile, a kind of

175

purposely bright yet sliding-away smile.

"Oh," she said, then repeated the "oh" again, as if she was starting over. "Oh, we ladies are getting together and sewing for an orphanage."

"You're kidding," I said. Mom can do a lot of things, but sew she cannot. My mom does things for charity, too, but never after school, because it's then, she says, that charity begins at home.

Such a lame excuse I never heard before. Sewing!

So maybe Mom was beginning to live her own life. I watched her suspiciously. I certainly didn't want a thing like that happening. I wanted Mom living *our* lives, as she'd always done.

I talked it over with that thick-domed brother of mine. "What's so far-out about Mom going away from the house once in a while?" he said, walking away fast so I had to run after him, which I hate to do. "You makin' a federal case out of it? Maybe she just wants to take off for a change."

"No, no," I argued and finally grabbed him by the arm. We were on our way to school, and if there's one thing neither of us wants to do, it's walk *together* to school. It makes you look as if you haven't any friends except your *brother!* You know?

This time he wasn't my brother, and I wasn't his sister. We were just two people with a problem, except he didn't think so.

"It's different from her *wanting* to be away," I tried to explain tensely. "She *looks* different. Nervous, kind of. And she *acts* different. She doesn't yell at us to do something all the time. Instead, she goes right ahead and does the things we're supposed to be yelled into doing. She doesn't even tell me to change my school clothes, which, as you well know, I don't do without being told. Or get to studying. Or set the table. Or help with dinner." I was half crying at that point. I *missed* it—the being told to do things I didn't do without being told. It seemed as if I were just floating aimlessly around in life.

"So what's to complain about?" Jerry said, in his usual smarty teen-age fashion.

"I don't like it," I whimpered. "It isn't natural."

Then I went on to point out the fact that Daddy didn't shout at us, either. He didn't even seem to notice us much anymore. He was too busy noticing Mom and asking if he could do something for her and wanting her to sit down.

"So?" countered Jerry, his tone exasperatingly indifferent.

He couldn't see anything wrong, and that was the whole idea. What *was* wrong? Things were *almost* the same. There was only a hint of a change, but it was a pretty big hint: Mom being gone every afternoon until just in time to fix dinner, laughing just as much as she always had but with a different tone in it, Daddy not laughing at all, and neither of them jumping on Jerry and me. I had a feeling that Mom didn't jump because she'd given up on us and that Daddy didn't because she'd told him not to. I was mixed up in my mind, and it made me cross.

That's what Gordy Beauchamp told me that day. Gordy's the one I go with. I don't say "steady," because I'm not allowed to go steady yet, but he's the only one, anyway. "What's eatin' you, Debbie?" he asked. "You're as cross as a bear."

"I am not," I answered.

"Sure you are. You almost bit my head off. And, say, how about it? How about me comin' over to your house after school, with your mom not there and all, huh? You said you'd think about it. Remember?"

"I have thought about it," I snapped, "and you can't come."

I was as surprised as Gordy, treating him that way. He went clomping down the hall, and I wouldn't have been surprised if he asked Shirley for a date—and she my best friend.

But my mind simply wouldn't stay on Gordy for long. First I was sorry I'd snapped at him, then glad I told him he couldn't come to the house when Mom wasn't there, then mad because Shirley would probably grab a date with him faster than he could ask for it. But then things at home began to worry me once more. I worried until I felt so miserable that I asked to be excused the rest of the afternoon.

All the way home, I wondered if Mom would be there, or had she already gone out for what she went out for every single day?

Well, her car was in the driveway, so I guessed she left later than this. I slipped in the side door and into my room, feeling pretty sorry for myself, I guess, and wanting to kind of hunch up in a ball and not think. Then I heard her voice from the front hall.

Was someone with her? I sat straight up on the bed, listening with all my might. Finally I

179

figured that she must be on the telephone, and quicker than thought, I picked up my extension from the bedside table, very, very carefully. So it's wrong to listen in on people's telephone conversations? Okay, it's wrong. But I'm glad I did. Even wishing I didn't know what I learned, I'm glad I learned it that terrible day.

It was Daddy's voice at the other end. ". . . just wanted to make sure you're all right. Almost ready to go for the treatment?"

Treatment? I thought. *What treatment?*

"Yes," Mom answered, her voice chipper but a little tired around the edges. Like a cake, you know? High in the middle but sloping at the sides. "Yes, I was just ready to leave the house."

"Now, be careful," Daddy said. People say "be careful" all the time, not even thinking about it. The way Daddy said it, you could tell he wanted to wrap Mom in cotton wool—it was that kind of "be careful." Then he sighed. "I wish that hospital was closer. Be careful of the traffic."

"Why?" Mom said, then laughed with a catch in her throat, as if she were laughing at a sick joke.

I began to get really scared then. Treatment . . . hospital . . . and the strange sound of their voices—not a mother-voice or a father-voice but a wife-and-husband voice, all pushed in together, knowing something, knowing everything.

"Why?" Daddy repeated her question, horrified. "Because I want to keep you—" he slowed —"I want to keep you for as long as I can."

"Yes," Mom said. "I'm sorry. I want to stay as long as I can, too. I'll be careful."

My hand perspired against the phone. I knew. At least, I almost knew what they knew—but not quite.

"I'd better leave now," Mom said. "There's the traffic you talked about, then the X-ray therapy and the rest afterward. I must leave so I can get back as soon as possible. I hate being gone too long after the children come home from school."

I didn't move. I held my breath and waited for something I didn't want to hear. I almost knew.

"Yes," Daddy said, "I suppose so. I wish you'd tell the children. They could help, you know. Take a load off you. I wish you'd let me tell them."

"No!" Mom's voice was explosive. "No! Think what it would do to them, knowing their mother hasn't long to live!" Her voice broke then for the first time. I dropped flat on the bed, the phone still glued to my ear, my other hand pressed tight against my mouth. "I won't have it," Mom said, almost angrily. "I won't allow them to bear such a burden until it's necessary, and it may not be necessary until the very last. The X-ray doctor says. . . ."

I dropped the phone on the bed and hunched against the pillow, holding my face in my hands, tight, tight, tight.

From far away, I heard Mom's heels tap-tapping along the front hall, just as if she were well and going to live a long, long time. I heard the front door close and then the sound of the motor. The car roared out of the driveway and turned down the street.

I lay still on my bed, wanting to die.

I heard the click of the refrigerator as it turned on and the hum of the air conditioner. I heard a dry leaf blow along the walk outside. Suddenly I knew I would have to carry this burden I had accidentally lifted—the one Mom wanted to keep from me. I would have to carry it well and silently and in a way that would help her. I slammed the awful phone back on the cradle, then settled it gently.

I got up and changed my school clothes for jeans and an old blouse. Then I picked up everything in my room. Just to do it right, I brought in the vacuum and cleaned the floor.

I hurried. I raced through the house looking for things to do. I found some ironing all dampened down and set up the ironing board. *I'm not very good at it, but I'll learn*, I thought.

Jerry came home from school. "Get out there and mow the lawn," I yelled.

"Who says?" he yelled back.

"I say," I answered, yelling again.

"Knock it off."

I set the iron down and almost told him. I opened my mouth to say, "Our mother is dying, and you're going to work as you've never worked before, and I'm going to work, too. We're going to give her all the love and consideration we owe her, which is plenty." But I didn't say it. I remembered how terribly Mom didn't want us to know, and if she could find the courage to hide it, I could find the courage to keep it hidden.

"Go out and mow the lawn," I said gently, "and I'll give you a quarter of my allowance. Okay?"

"Okay!" he said, surprised at my generosity.

I had just started dinner when Mom came home. I wanted to rush into her arms and have her comfort me the way she used to last year, when I was just a child. But I wasn't a child anymore, so I just stood still instead and really looked at her. I guess people don't really look at their moms very much, because when I looked at mine that day, I saw how thin she had become and that her face had a yellow tinge to it, as if it were white paper that had been left in the sunshine.

"Why, Debbie," she cried, surprised, "you've started dinner!"

"Sure," I said and yanked the lettuce from the refrigerator.

"And done the ironing!"

"I thought I might as well," I said.

"Well! Well, Debbie, how nice!" She looked around, as if she couldn't believe her eyes. "Why?"

I stopped myself again from falling into her arms and telling her how sorry I was and to please help me bear this burden she didn't want me to bear. "Gosh, Mom," I said, "I don't know. Maybe I've just grown up, huh? Maybe I'm not a typical teen-ager anymore. You wouldn't want

me to be a typical teen-ager forever, would
you?"

"No, dear, not forever," she said.

And that's when the sob caught right in the
middle of my throat and stuck. It's still there. I
guess I'll just have to work around it, because
it's part of the burden and the secret I carry—
and a part of growing up fast, so my mom can
see how I'll be and not have to worry about
that, at least.

No Boy. I'm a Girl!

M. J. Amft

IN THE MIDDLE of my junior year, I became a
civilian rights agitator. Not civil rights—that's
no problem in our town—but civilian rights.
School wasn't the army, right? They didn't own
us, right? They couldn't put us in uniform.
Soldiers had to wear GI clothes and GI hair-
cuts, and polish their buttons and shoes, but
this was *civilian* life, a high school in a free
country, and they suspended three boys for wearing blue jeans to school. Actually, they just sent
them home and told them to come back wearing
something else, but it was the principle of the
thing that mattered to me.

I kept thinking about it all afternoon, getting

madder and madder. What if those boys were so poor they didn't have anything else to wear? Are the poor to be punished? Is that democracy? Is that the Great Society? I happened to know that those particular three boys weren't poor, but what if they had been?

"It's the principle of the thing," I said. I was walking home with Allen Newman, the way I always did because (for one) he lived at the end of my block and (for two) I had a hopeless crush on him—hopeless, because girls meant absolutely nothing in Allen's life. Clothes meant nothing to him, either. He wore plain, conservative, utilitarian clothes that his mother ordered from a catalogue. She took his measurements and sent away for plain white shirts and plain dark wash pants. He had one lightweight windbreaker, one heavy windbreaker (both dark blue), one dark blue suit (which he never wore), one raincoat (which he never wore), and three neckties. When his shoes wore out, he went to Clark's Shoe Shop and asked for "a pair of the same"—brown moccasins. Every second Saturday, he went to the barber and had his hair trimmed, and he refused to wear the cologne his grandmother gave him, the aftershave lotion his aunt gave him, or the Aphrodisia I gave him. He hated perfume for men.

The reason I knew all these intimate things about Allen, and the reason I gave him a Christmas present, is that his mother and mine are longtime best friends, who are always on the telephone, talking about their children.

My mother was on the phone that day when I got home. "Just be glad you don't have a daughter—speaking of which, here she is. Good-bye, Ruthie. I'll call you tomorrow. Tell Allen I'm very proud he got another A."

"That was Ruthie Newman," she said. "Allen got another A."

"I know. Listen, Mother, there's something terrible going on at our school. Allen doesn't care, because he has absolutely no feeling of civic responsibility, but I think it's criminal. I'm sure it's illegal."

"Drugs!" my mother said. "Airplane glue? Or worse?"

"No, no. It's the school authorities. It's the principal, actually, Mr. Hayden. I mean he *is* the school authority. He's the one."

"Mr. Hayden is pushing drugs!"

"Mother, will you listen, please? Nobody said

189

anything about drugs. Mr. Hayden is saying you can't wear blue jeans to school."

"Why should I wear blue jeans to school? Much as I hate those PTA meetings, when I do go, I wear my good black suit. Where did Mr. Hayden get the idea I wanted to wear blue jeans?"

You see how it is with my mother? She's very emotional, and she jumps to conclusions. I finally managed to explain that by "you" I meant "one," or three: the three boys in the blue jeans. I didn't think any public school or any principal had the right to dictate to any student in regard to personal appearance, and I thought all parents should write a protest letter.

My mother wasn't interested and changed the subject. "Are you going out with that ugly Roger tomorrow night?" she asked.

When I told her no, that the thing with Roger was all over, she was glad; but when Ralph showed up, she dragged me into the kitchen and said, "For months you dated a boy who needed a good dermatologist. Now it's a boy who needs an orthodontist. What's wrong with their parents? Where do you find these boys whose mothers neglect them? Why can't you find a nice boy whose parents take an interest in his welfare, a boy like Allen?"

Why indeed? I was willing. Meantime, I didn't want to spend weekends doing chemistry experiments. That's what Allen did. He had all these smelly things in the basement, which really bugged his mother. As Ruthie said, maybe daughters washed their hair so much it clogged up the drains, but at least daughters didn't cause terrible smells to come up through the hot-air registers. To which, of course, my mother replied that smells in the basement result in A's in chemistry, whereas hair in the drains results in nothing but a plumber's bill.

I didn't think Ralph was anything much, myself—but he was a date, he was a way to get out on Saturday nights, and he agreed with me about the blue jeans.

On Monday morning, every homeroom teacher had a mimeographed "Memo From the Principal's Office," which was read aloud and then stuck on the bulletin board:

> No boy shall be allowed to wear blue jeans during school hours or while in the school building. Unobservance of this rule shall meet with immediate suspension.

191

I don't think Mr. Hayden is literate. "Unobservance"? Is that a word? And what right had he? What right?

On the way home, I fumed about it to Allen, who said there was no reason for me to get excited. Why should I concern myself over what boys couldn't wear, as long as I was allowed to wear what I pleased?

"Because if one group's rights are infringed upon, another group's rights are in danger." And then I screamed and hugged him—which I did every now and then, being unable to restrain myself, but he never reacted, one way or the other—and said, "You've given me a great idea! I'm a girl!"

"I thought you knew that," he said.

I ignored that, because I had suddenly realized the right way to protest. Not with letters and petitions, not with marches and sit-ins . . . the way to protest was to take Mr. Hayden's directive word for word, but *only* word for word. The letter killeth. Aha! "No *boy*," it said. I'm a girl.

Of course, I knew my mother wasn't going to let me wear blue jeans to school. As it was, one of her big complaints about me was my clothes. She hates colored stockings, textured stockings, fake fur, vinyl, wild colors, dots, stripes, and patterns, except "a nice, soft herringbone or a muted plaid." She had a running lecture on what a pretty girl I could be if I would wear a nice tweed skirt, a cashmere sweater, a string of small pearls, and nylons. Fashionwise, she lives in the past.

I'd never get out of my own house in blue jeans, but Ruthie Newman slept late mornings, and Harry, Allen's father, left very early, so Allen was the only one up and around, and I could stuff jeans in my book bag and change at his house. The trouble was that if I told him about my plan, he might say no. So I simply asked him if he would let me use his powder room the next morning.

"I don't want to wake your mother," I said, "so I won't ring the bell. I'll just whistle two bars of *Help!* through the kitchen keyhole. You'll be out there eating your cereal, and you'll hear me and let me in."

Allen eats six bowls of cold cereal every morning. He will not eat "a good hot breakfast," which is why Ruthie sleeps late. What mother wants to torture herself watching a growing boy eat nothing but bowl after bowl of cold cereal,

193

when she would be only too glad to cook him some eggs and bacon?

Allen is shy. He started to say, "Why do you want to use our—" and then gulped and blushed, which was what I was counting on.

The next morning, I whistled at the keyhole. Allen let me in, looked embarrassed, and poured out another bowl of Crispy Critters, while I slipped into the powder room and my blue jeans.

As we walked along to school, I said, "Don't you notice anything about me?"

Of course he hadn't. Allen never noticed anything about anybody. That was another thing that bugged Ruthie, who said he was only interested in *things*, not people, that there was something abnormal about him because he didn't seem to be aware of other people; he didn't *relate*. To which my mother said, "Be glad. Debbie is aware of other people. Debbie relates. And to whom? Stupid boys and boys with dandruff."

But as soon as I got to homeroom, wow! Mrs. Saunders gave me a talk on how she was a teacher, hired to teach, not to discipline. I could march right down and present myself to Mr. Hayden as *his* problem. I was really kind of scared. I'd never been sent to the principal's office, but I kept telling myself it was the principle that really mattered, so the heck with the principal—and his office.

Mr. Hayden exploded. You'd have thought I was wearing a bikini. I just kept looking gee-gosh-I'm-just-a-little-girl bewildered, and when he finally ran out of steam, I said, "Gee, Mr. Hayden, sir, I sure am sorry, but your directive specifically stated 'No *boy.*' I'm a *girl.*"

I stuck out my chest, which is only 32A but enough to get the idea over. Mr. Hayden closed his eyes and clenched his teeth and fists.

"And you can't send me home," I said, "because there's nobody there, and I don't have a key, and the temperature is below freezing, twenty-nine degrees, humidity fifty percent, barometer—"

Mr. Hayden opened everything: eyes, teeth, fists, and the door to the outer office.

"Miss Nussbaum!" he screamed. "Take a memo! . . . No boy and no girl, no man and no woman, shall be allowed to wear blue jeans during school hours or while in the school building. Unobservance of this rule shall meet with immediate suspension."

195

The next day I was a big hero with the original three blue jean boys. I hadn't even known them to talk to, but they all stopped me in the hall and told me I was the greatest and they really appreciated what I had done for them. I said I hadn't done it for them. I had done it for all free people, all civilians.

"Yesterday the armed forces, today the schools, tomorrow the world. It's not 1984 yet," I said, "and I'm not through fighting! I've got new ammunition now."

When they asked me if I was going to wear blue jeans anyway and get suspended, I told them about my plan. It made them so happy they all introduced themselves and invited me to have a cola at the Snackaroo: Paul, Chris, and Peter. They were all quite cute—not as cute as Allen but cute enough to impress Mary Jo and Cathy, who were in the Snackaroo and at loose ends. I'm not at all convinced that Mary Jo and Cathy really had civilian rights in their hearts, but they were more than willing to join the protest.

The next morning, I whistled two bars of *Help!* into Allen's keyhole. He opened the door and whispered, "I didn't know you were going to be coming here *every* morning."

I looked at him with my quiet-desperation look, and he said, "Uh, it's right down the hall to your left" and poured out a bowl of Alpha Bits. He still didn't notice anything until we got to school and Mrs. Saunders turned pale purple and sent Paul, Chris, Peter, Mary Jo, Cathy, and me down to Mr. Hayden's office. We were all wearing wheat jeans.

"Now, let me do the talking," I said, "and remember not to look defiant or sullen."

Paul, Chris, and Peter—who had spent years standing in front of the mirror getting those eyebrows right *down* there, man, right in the old eye socket, cool—opened wide and grinned.

"No, no!" I said. *"Not* 'What—me worry?' Look *innocent* and bewildered." It's not easy to learn my gee-gosh look in one hurried lesson on your way to the guillotine, but they tried, and they did keep their mouths shut.

Mr. Hayden opened his, and when he had to inhale after a ten-minute rant, I quickly said, "Gee, Mr. Hayden, sir, the directive plainly says, right there in black and white, *blue.*"

"Young lady," he said, "I don't know what your game is, but you're not going to win."

The new memo had to be altered several times. Its original form was:

> No boy and no man (except school janitors and repairmen) shall wear jeans or cowboy pants or work pants of any kind or color during school hours or while in the school building. Furthermore, at these same times and in this same place, no girl or woman shall wear any kind of pants.

"Mrs. Saunders," I said, "I do not believe that the mothers of this community want their daughters to go to school without any kind of pants. I believe that if the press obtained the information that a high school principal was forbidding the girls to wear underwear—"

Bedlam, of course. Mrs. Saunders flounced out of the room, while everybody cheered and whistled for me—except Allen, who was using the free time to work on an assignment for extra credit.

Of course, Mr. Hayden's next effort, "No girl shall wear any *visible* pants," was a mistake that even as confused a writer as Mr. Hayden shouldn't have made. After a greal deal of hilarity in the halls ("But I don't own any *invisible* pants; does that mean visible to the naked

eyes, sir?"), a monitor was dispatched, on Mr. Hayden's orders, to rip down all memos. But he hadn't surrendered.

The following Monday there was a new one. He must have labored on it all weekend:

> In the school and on school grounds or property, boys (unless engaged in legitimate and authorized athletics) shall wear, at all times, trousers or slacks or wash pants (not jeans, cowboy pants, or work pants). The slacks or pants or trousers shall not be cut off or torn off or folded or rolled up. Boys shall also wear shirts or sweaters. Girls shall wear dresses or skirts and blouses or skirts and sweaters. No other form of clothing will be tolerated. Underwear shall be concealed.

"That about ties it up," Chris said. "Now what are you going to do?"

"I'm going to keep fighting," I said. "Civilian rights shall not perish."

That evening I asked my mother if I could wear that jumper to school—the nice royal blue one she bought me for Christmas.

"Well, of course!" she said. "Debbie, I'd love it! I shopped all over, and it *hangs* there."

"Can I wear the shirt with the button-down collar?"

"You'll look adorable! Why, a girl with lovely—"

"You'll have to write a note, Mom, and I don't even know if that will work. You may have to get a lot of outside support. Mr. Hayden has absolutely forbidden any girl to wear anything except a dress or a skirt and blouse or sweater."

That did it. My mother leaped to the bait like a starving trout. That lovely jumper, that sweet little shirt. Was Mr. Hayden crazy? First she called Ruthie, then she called everyone she knew in the PTA; eventually, of course, she got Mrs. Franklin, who talks even louder and faster than my mother and therefore got a word in edgewise. Several words, in fact, like *Debbie*, *blue jeans*, and *wheat jeans*.

"An utter untruth!" my mother said. "I am here every morning to see to it that my daughter is properly dressed. Never has she left this house on a school morning in jeans. Kooky things, yes. Green stockings, nouveau art, London look, baby doll, mod, rock, pop, op. I'll admit she's done everything to look like a freak, even though she is really a very pretty girl, if she would only take my advice and—"

But it was Mrs. Franklin's turn to tell how her

Bonnie was also a lovely girl, who never lied to her mother and certainly was not a trouble-maker or talebearer, but who said positively that. . . .

When my mother hung up, she looked at me.

"It's true, Mom," I said. "I changed at Allen's house."

"*Allen* suggested this to you?"

"No, Mom. It wasn't his fault. He just let me use the powder room."

By that time, she had Ruthie on the phone again, and for a while I thought a lifelong friendship was going to end right there. But pretty soon a new, purring note crept into her voice.

"You know, he might be beginning to relate, Ruthie. I mean, he's bound to begin to become aware someday, and remember that terrible girl who kept making eyes at him last year? In the alley, when he took out the garbage? What if he relates to somebody like that? A girl like that in your powder room, and Allen could become a 'changed boy. For the worse. It might even affect his grades, and you know Harry will kill himself if Allen doesn't get into Harvard. Well, I'd be very happy if Debbie and Allen became interested in each other, but I doubt it. Who has that kind of luck? Girls only want to go out with boys who come from terrible families. Be glad you don't have a daughter."

The PTA got in on it then, and so did the student council and the local newspaper. Everybody had conflicting opinions. There were mothers (of daughters) demanding that all boys wear suit jackets to school; dressed like gentlemen, they would act like gentlemen. Whereupon a mother screeched that her son grew six inches in six weeks, and she was not going to be stuck with a lot of expensive, outgrown suit jackets. There was a compromise suggestion that all boys wear ties, but that was voted down when someone explained that it had been tried at another school and the boys wore the ties around their waists or ankles.

"All boys wear ties around necks" resulted in ties being wound around and around like a choker. "All boys wear ties under collars and tied." They tied them in the back. One lady got up and said that in this temperature zone there was a problem, but no clothes meant no uniforms! No uniforms meant no war. Her family was from the South, and if there had been no boys in blue or in gray, if all had been dressed only in the skin God gave them, there would have been no war. *All* clothes were unnatural.

The controversy went on for months. When there was a memo: "No girl's skirt shall be more than two inches above the kneecap," I dutifully dragged out my last year's granny dress and shuffled off, in sure anticipation of a new memo: "No girl's skirt shall be more than three inches below the kneecap."

But my heart wasn't in it anymore. I didn't really care at all. All I really cared about was Allen. I didn't just have a crush on him. I really *liked* that Allen. He kept getting bigger and cuter every day. Those cold cereal commercials don't lie. Sugar Dots and Frosty B's were giving him muscles and rosy cheeks. Even though he spent all his time studying or doing homework or smelling up the basement, while his mother begged him to please, please get a little fresh air, he kept blossoming. And I was going out on Saturday with Randy, whom I hated.

By now it was almost the end of the school year, and Mr. Hayden had washed his hands of the whole thing. His final memo was "Anybody can wear anything. What do I care?" Mr. Hayden was cracking up, but so was I. Every Saturday night, when my mother came up and said, "He's here. He's waiting down there in that furry vest, with his skinny bare arms," I shuddered. For a rock singer, okay, but I really wished Randy would wear a nice soft herringbone or muted plaid, something that would blend into the background, so you wouldn't notice how ugly he was. He also wore a toothpick in the corner of his mouth. He said something about how it kept him from smoking.

I had almost forgotten about the civilian rights fight, and so had everybody else except Mr. Hayden, a sore loser, who decided to get back at me. At the last day assembly, right in front of the entire junior class, Mr. Hayden took his last shot.

"To those of you who doubted that there is a correlation between conservative dress and scholastic achievement, I would like to point out that no boys with long hair and barefoot sandals made the honor list. And Miss Debbie Markam, the first girl to enter these halls of learning wearing blue jeans, and who has consistently advocated and agitated for extremes in styles, has received a final grade of C-minus in advanced algebra, which certainly keeps her out of the upper ten percent. Contrariwise, the top student in the class, a boy with straight A's, has managed to maintain his fine school record under the so-called dictatorial militarism of my original directive asking for a degree of prudence and decorum in personal appearance. Allen Newman, please stand up."

That's when Mr. Hayden lost the fight. The last thing Allen wanted to do was stand up in the assembly hall, but Mrs. Saunders kept poking and hissing at him. Mr. Hayden said, "Look at him. Our top student. And what is he wearing? Clean cut!" Everyone looked at Allen, and Allen looked at the floor. I felt Mr. Hayden had made a mistake there, but I didn't know how big a one.

On the way home, Allen said, "Mr. Hayden is a boob! First of all, it was a real achievement for you to get a C-minus in advanced algebra. If he knew anything about education, he would have known you have a definite math block, probably developed from incorrect teaching in the formative years. Next, no one has the right to force someone to stand up in the middle of assembly and be stared at just because he's not wearing a furry vest!"

"Well, Allen, he was really asking you to stand up because of the A's."

"That's no excuse. People have the right to be the way they want to be, without being pointed out. It's the principle of the thing!"

Allen spent the summer in the country at his grandmother's. He was killing several birds with that stone. He was growing sunflowers to prove some sort of involved thing about seed pods, number ratio, and phototropism. I couldn't understand it, but, whatever it was, he proved it. He was making his grandmother deliriously happy, because she's crazy about him. He was making his mother happy, because he was getting a lot of fresh air and because she had a chance to clean out their basement.

I got rid of Randy and spent a dull summer baby-sitting, lying on the beach, and trying to sit on my hair. It was everybody's ambition: hair so long you could sit on it. I never made it. By the end of August, I was so bored with everybody's measuring and measuring that I had the whole works chopped off, except for some thick bangs and sideburns. My mother fainted.

Since she was sitting on our down-filled sofa

207

at the time, it wasn't very much of a faint, and in about two minutes she was up and on the phone with Ruthie.

"You know how I begged her to get a haircut? This is my payment for opening my mouth. Just be glad you don't have a daughter."

A week before school started, Allen came home. Then Ruthie fainted. She called my mother, and my mother dashed over, and I dashed along with her because I couldn't believe it! Allen?

"Debbie," he said, "I like your haircut. The back of your neck is very sexy looking."

He asked me to go to a movie with him and said he wanted to go places all week long so he could get used to people staring at him. He wanted to be in full control of his emotions when school started. He kept giving me little hugs right from the start, and by the end of the week —well, Allen was relating.

The first day of school he called for me, and we walked off, hand in hand. I was wearing a brown skirt and a crisp white blouse. He was in brown slacks and a white shirt. We both looked nice and neat, our hair clean and shiny. His was about eight inches longer than mine, hanging down around his shoulders. It was the principle of the thing. He had decided that Mr. Hayden had no scientific basis for the assumption that long hair or sandals led to low marks or that blue jeans were the cause of a continuing math block in the female.

"I intend to prove to Mr. Hayden that I can be an A student without ever getting a haircut. But I'm nervous! Stick by me, Debbie."

I was willing. Mr. Hayden was standing at the main entrance, welcoming the students. When Allen shook his hand and said, "Good morning, sir. Nice to be back," Mr. Hayden's lips started to tremble. He turned pale, and his eyes rolled back, but he didn't faint. He just turned slowly away and walked into his office, a defeated man. I almost felt sorry for him, except that when it comes to something as important as civilian rights, you've got to be strong. After all, we only have a few years to fight before 1984.

Acknowledgments

"GOOD-BYE, MISS KITTY" by Jane L. Sears, previously unpublished, published with permission of Elyse Sommer, Inc., acting for the author.

"DOG-SITTER" by Carl Henry Rathjen, previously unpublished. By permission of the author and Larry Sternig Literary Agency.

"FLY FREE" by Carol S. Adler. Copyright 1970 by *American Girl*. Appeared originally in *American Girl*, March, 1970. Reprinted by permission of the *American Girl*, a magazine for all girls, published by the Girl Scouts of the U.S.A.

"A PERSON, AFTER ALL" by Constance Kwolek. Copyright 1970 by *American Girl*. Appeared originally in *American Girl*, April, 1970. Reprinted by permission of the *American Girl*, a magazine for all girls, published by the Girl Scouts of the U.S.A.

"TWO NICE GIRLS" by Frances Gray Patton. Reprinted by permission of Russell & Volkening, Inc., and *Seventeen*® Magazine. Copyright © 1964 by Triangle Publications, Inc.